WORDS ON BATHROOM WALLS

WORDS

BATH

W

ON
ROOM
ALLS

Julia Walton

RANDOM HOUSE 🏠 NEW YORK

Text copyright © 2017 by Julia Walton
Jacket and interior photographs copyright © by Jamie Farrant/Getty Images;
Roberto Trivella/EyeEm/Getty Images

All rights reserved. Published in the United States
by Random House Children's Books,
a division of Penguin Random House LLC, New York.

Random House and the colophon are registered trademarks
of Penguin Random House LLC.

Visit us on the Web! randomhouseteens.com

Educators and librarians, for a variety of teaching tools,
visit us at RHTeachersLibrarians.com

Library of Congress Cataloging-in-Publication Data
Names: Walton, Julia, 1986– author.
Title: Words on bathroom walls / Julia Walton.
Description: First edition. | New York : Random House, [2017] |
Summary: "Adam is a recently diagnosed schizophrenic and journals
to his therapist about family, friends, and first loves as he undergoes
a new drug trial for the mental illness that allows him to keep his secret
for only so long"—Provided by publisher.
Identifiers: LCCN 2016017419 | ISBN 978-0-399-55088-1 (hardback) |
ISBN 978-0-399-55089-8 (lib. bdg.) | ISBN 978-0-399-55090-4 (ebook)
Subjects: | CYAC: Schizophrenia—Fiction. | Mental illness—Fiction. |
Dating (Social customs—Fiction.
Classification: LCC PZ7.1.W3642 Wo 2017 | DDC [Fic]—dc23

Printed in the United States of America
10 9 8 7 6 5 4 3 2 1
First Edition

Random House Children's Books supports the First Amendment
and celebrates the right to read.

For Dougie,
who holds my hand so I don't get lost

WORDS ON BATHROOM WALLS

INITIAL DOSAGE: 0.5 mg. Adam Petrazelli, 16 years old, is a subject of the clinical trial for ToZaPrex. He is reluctant to engage during therapy sessions. Nonverbal communication only. Not uncommon, given his reluctance to participate in therapy aspect of the drug trial.

AUGUST 15, 2012

My first doctor said it was unusual for the symptoms to manifest in someone so young. Schizophrenic males are more commonly diagnosed in their early to late twenties. I remember thinking, *Well, shit, that's awesome. I'm unusual.*

I'm probably not supposed to swear in these entries. Shit.

But you did say to treat them as confidential and that they would never be used against me, so I don't see any reason why I shouldn't use whatever language I'm comfortable with. I'm also not going to worry about ending sentences with a preposition. Or starting sentences with a conjunction. If this is, as you put it, "a safe space for me to express myself," then I'm going to write what I'm thinking exactly as I'm thinking it.

I'll answer your questions, but I won't do it during our sessions. I'll do it here, on paper, where I can look at what I write before I hand it over to you. So I can edit what you see, and avoid saying anything that might get me kicked out of the drug trial.

I don't always say the things I mean to say when I talk to someone. It's impossible to swallow words after letting them out, so it's better for me not to speak at all if I can help it. You'll just have to deal with that.

But I get that you have questions about my illness. Once people find out, it's all they can talk about. You probably know that it's the reason my mom and stepdad picked you. Because you have experience.

Fair enough. I've got to say you handled it pretty well. There were maybe two minutes of silence before you handed me a notepad and told me to write about our sessions afterward if I didn't want to talk, which I don't. And it's not because I don't want to get better—it's because I don't want to be here. More specifically, I don't want this to be real. I'd like to treat therapy the way I treat everything else I'd like to ignore. Like it doesn't exist. Because I already know that being here isn't going to fix anything. The drug might, though.

You asked me when I first noticed that something was not quite normal. A change of some kind.

In the beginning I thought it was my glasses. No, not glasses. Spectacles. I like that word better.

I got them when I turned twelve because I couldn't stop squinting and it drove my mom nuts. Dr. Leung is the one doctor I actually like, because he fixed a problem by giving me something fairly simple. Spectacles.

Problem solved. I could see and my mom was happy.

But that was also when I realized I was seeing things other people couldn't see. I was the only one jerking my head or squinting my eyes to get a better look. Everyone else was looking at *me*, not the birds that flew through the open window or the strange people who just sort of appeared in the living room. So I stopped wearing my spectacles and told my mom I'd lost them. For a while that worked and I could pretend, but eventually, she bought so many pairs there was no excuse. I was screwed.

I didn't tell her I was seeing things for a long time. She'd just married my stepdad and they were happy. When I did finally tell her, it was because I didn't have a choice. The principal called, and when Mom hung up the phone, she looked at me as if she were seeing me for the first time.

"Mrs. Brizeno said you looked up in the chemistry

lab, started screaming, and fell to the floor." I remember how calm she was. My mom has this Jedi voice that sort of washes over you when she's trying to get information. "What did you see?"

I didn't answer her right away. I took off my spectacles and tried to pretend she wasn't there, that she had faded out of the room after asking the question. I'm good at making myself believe these things, but it was harder this time. She just stood there, waiting for an answer.

"Bats," I said, looking down at my shoes. "Huge black bats."

I didn't tell her that they were twice the size of regular bats or that they had human eyes or that their tiny fangs hung like needles from their mouths.

When she started crying, I wished the bats had been real. That the creepy little bastards had eaten me in the chemistry lab and I'd never had to see the way my mom looked at me in that moment: like I was crazy.

I really didn't want to be crazy. Nobody *wants* to be crazy, but now that I know what's happening to me, now that I understand what's going on in my head, I don't want to think about what it means to know you're crazy. To know that your family knows you're crazy.

My stepdad, Paul, is a nice guy. He's good for my mom. They dated for years before they got married, and he always made the effort to keep up with my life, ask me about school, etc. He's an attorney who can give her the things she's had to do without since my dad left.

Now that he knows about me, about the *illness,* things are different. He doesn't know what to do with me anymore. We'll still sit and watch TV, but I can almost hear him thinking when I'm in the room. The weirdest feeling, aside from seeing things that aren't actually there, is sitting on the couch next to a grown man who is suddenly afraid of me. He didn't used to be afraid. It's hard not to take that personally.

What am *I* afraid of? Pass. I'm sure you'll figure it out soon enough.

The good thing is that he actually does love my mom. And since my mom loves me, he makes an effort. He was the one who suggested the new private school instead of tossing me back into a school where all the kids knew there was something wrong with me.

In two weeks, I start my junior year at St. Agatha's. It's a K–12 school. My mom and Paul made the staff aware of my "condition," and because it's Catholic, they can't exactly turn me away. That would be pretty hypocritical. From what I know about the guy, Jesus wouldn't turn me away.

Paul also made sure that my new school knows not to talk about my illness. As a lawyer, he explained that *legally* they aren't allowed to tell anyone what I have, which I appreciate.

It's hard starting as a junior in a new school. It's significantly more difficult to make friends when people know you see things you shouldn't be able to see.

DOSAGE: 0.5 mg. Same dosage. Adam still unwilling to speak.

AUGUST 22, 2012

I became an expert on my condition the second I was diagnosed. I can tell anyone who wants to know all the drugs, the most recent studies, the positive and negative symptoms. When I say "positive" and "negative," I don't mean "good" and "bad." It basically all sucks.

"Positive" refers to symptoms *caused* by the disorder. Like delusions.

"Negative" symptoms are *reduced* by the disorder. Like lack of initiative and motivation.

There really is no clear path for the disease to travel. Some people have visions. Some people hear voices. And some people just get paranoid. My mom would also want me to take a minute to tell you about the huge strides in medicine to help people cope with the side effects. She's a glass-half-full kind of woman.

The whole seeing and hearing things that other people can't is like something straight out of Harry Potter. Like in *The Chamber of Secrets* when he heard the voice through the walls. Keeping it a secret made me feel privileged, like waiting for my letter from Hogwarts to arrive. I thought maybe it would mean something.

But then Ron ruins that possibility when he says, "Hearing voices no one else can hear isn't a good sign, even in the wizarding world." Harry ended up being fine. Nobody sent him to therapy or tried to give him pills. He just got to live in a world where everything he thought he'd heard and seen turned out to be real. Lucky bastard.

I can't really complain about pills, though. Things have gotten better since I started the new drug. We won't know how it really affects me until I've been on the full dosage for a while. They're easing me into it, which you already know. Part of the reason I'm required to sit in your office once a week is so you can spot any problems and report back to the clinical trial doctors.

You asked what I know about my treatment. So I'll tell you all the stuff you already know. The drug is called ToZaPrex, which, according to the label, can cause, among other things, (1) decreased white blood cell count (which hinders the body's ability to combat disease),

(2) seizures, (3) severely low blood pressure, (4) dizziness, (5) trouble breathing, and (6) severe headaches.

My doctors have assured my mother that the worst side effects are really rare. And not to worry. Ha. Yeah. Don't worry.

I've experienced some of the side effects. Headaches mostly. The kind that sort of nest in your brain and throb for a while until they get bored and leave you alone. I don't feel compelled to act out everything that runs through my mind, which is nice. But it doesn't make the visions go away. I still see things I know I shouldn't be seeing. The difference is that I know I shouldn't be seeing them.

What do I see? Well, let's start with *who*. I see Rebecca. I know now that she isn't real because she never changes. She's beautiful and tall—like Amazon tall—with huge blue eyes and long hair that falls to her waist. And she's sweet and never says a word. As far as hallucinations go, she's completely harmless. I've only ever seen her cry once, the day my mom found out about me. When it happened, I still thought Rebecca was real. I didn't understand that she was crying *because* I was crying.

And no, Rebecca isn't the only one I see, but I don't like to talk about the others. The more I think about them, the more likely they are to appear, and they . . .

ruin things. It's like they wait for my mind to quiet down before they show up.

Anyway, the visions usually start with something small, something moving out of the corner of my eye or a voice that sounds familiar and then stays with me for hours. And sometimes it's just a feeling that someone somewhere is watching me, which I know is ridiculous. Why would anyone bother, right? But I still keep the blinds drawn. I don't really know why. I guess it's just the need for privacy. I'd like to, for once, feel properly alone.

A month ago, before I started taking ToZaPrex, I couldn't tell when I was slipping out of control. I would be afraid for no reason. Everything I saw was real to me. Once the hallucinations started, there was no switching them off. I could be lost in them for hours.

Now, when my mind starts misbehaving, I can at least watch its projections like a movie. Real CGI shit. Sometimes it's actually kind of beautiful. I can watch a whole field of grass erupt into a cloud of butterflies. Sometimes voices serenade me to sleep, and now that I know they're not real, I'm not afraid of them. So that's nice. It's the stuff that jumps out at me that makes me look like a spaz.

No, I'm not nervous about starting school.

I got my new uniform. White polo shirt, red wool vest

with school insignia, and butt-ugly navy-blue shorts that flare out from my waist and hang like elephant skin. And I've done all the required reading for my classes, so I guess I'm as ready as I'll ever be.

You know something, though? I honestly don't get how you can sit there, read my journal entries aloud, and then ask questions for an entire hour while I say nothing. That's weird. I'm crazy, and I think that's weird.

DOSAGE: 0.5 mg. Same dosage. Adam starts new school. Still unwilling to speak. Perhaps new environment will act as catalyst for progress in therapy.

AUGUST 29, 2012

It's pretty shitty to start school before Labor Day. I mean, like, really shitty. But I guess the first week back sucks no matter what. And it's not even over yet.

I don't have my driver's license, and I have no intention of getting it anytime soon because it just seems like one more thing I have to figure out and be responsible for. And it's just not worth it.

At my last school, I usually walked, but my mom insisted on driving me on my first day at St. Agatha's. There was something manic in the way she drove, like she wanted it to be casual but she was way too nervous to actually pull that off. But when we finally got to the line of cars outside school, she just smiled and said, "Have a good day." I could tell she wanted to kiss me goodbye, but once, when I was eight, I got mad at her for doing that in front of people, and she's restrained herself ever since. I wish I hadn't done that.

Pretty sure I just trudged out of the car with my backpack. I meant to smile at her reassuringly but forgot at the last minute. So she probably thought I was nervous when I actually wasn't.

You had questions about my first day. Let's focus on those, shall we?

You asked how it was different from my last school. It wasn't, really, aside from the uniforms. Everyone still looked miserable. No one was awake yet. And there was a definite feeling of *Why me?* So there was some solidarity in that, I suppose.

My first mission after finding my locker and putting my stuff down was to meet with my school ambassador, Ian Stone. Apparently, all new kids are assigned a school ambassador who is responsible for showing them the school and walking them to class. He was waiting in the front office when I got there, and I knew immediately that he was a douche. It wasn't the hair or the way he looked me up and down when we shook hands or the fact that he was chewing gum with his mouth open. It was just something about the air around him. It was like he was taking up more space than was strictly necessary.

His grin never quite reached his eyes as he scanned the room.

Sometimes it takes a while to get to know a person before you can tell what they're like, but he was easy to read. He was a collector of information.

I could tell by the way he made small talk with the old woman behind the front desk, asked about her kids, and took a handful of mints from the jar on the counter and casually stuffed them into his pocket. She smiled at him, and just as he was turning to leave, I saw him take the wad of gum out of his mouth and stick it under the counter.

Then he led me into the hall.

"So you'll need to pick up your PE uniform, and then you have bio, right?" he asked.

I nodded. There was a well-practiced laziness to the way he walked, like he was moving quickly but didn't care enough to be in a hurry. He pointed out a few buildings along the way and then gestured to a door off the side of the gym.

"I'll be out here when you're done," he said.

But when I came out with my gym clothes, he was gone. Can't say I was surprised. Not that I was unpopular or anything at my last school, but this guy just had a look about him like he was going to ditch me at the first opportunity. If I had to guess, I think he was disappointed that I don't look like someone he could easily manipulate.

I was kind of screwed because I had no idea where I was going. Classes hadn't started yet, so I was about to head back to the school office to get a map when a girl came out of a room to my left carrying a roll sheet marked for the office. She stopped in front of me with a quizzical look on her face.

"Are you lost?" she asked.

"I think so," I said, taking a second to register the fact that she was tiny, but also really pretty in an angry-hummingbird sort of way. She moved quickly with short, rapid, no-nonsense steps, but there was something graceful about her, too.

"Didn't they assign you an ambassador?" she asked, adjusting her glasses.

"Yeah, Ian Stone. But he—"

"Ditched you," she said, nodding. "Yeah, he does that. What's your first class?"

"Biology."

"This way," she said, leading me through a courtyard and up a flight of stairs. I stuffed my gym clothes into my backpack and followed her.

"So why is he like that?"

She looked at me like I'd just asked her the dumbest question she'd ever heard in her life. "His family makes huge donations to the school. All his brothers went here."

"So he's basically a legacy douche?" I asked. A smile flickered across her face.

"Something like that. Also, some people don't need a reason to be jerks. It comes naturally."

"Not to everyone," I whispered under my breath.

"*Most* people suck," she said, hearing me. "This is you." She nodded toward the door in front of us, but she was gone before I even had the chance to say thank you or get her name.

I wasn't the last one in the room, so it wasn't as awkward as it could've been when I sat down next to an impossibly pale guy with white knee-high socks. He was meticulously clean. His fingernails, his clothes, his skin. Everything about him was blindingly white, like he'd been dipped in Clorox. He immediately introduced himself as Dwight Olberman.

Once he'd said it, I knew he could have no other name. A stranger could have named him at the hospital, and that would have been the name they picked for him. I know Adam isn't the coolest name, either, but to be named Dwight and to really have it suit you—that's unfortunate. I think I'd go by my middle name in that case. Unless it's Cletus or something.

When we took roll, the nun at the front didn't make

me stand up and say a few things about myself, which was nice of her. The rest of the class just turned around and stared for a minute when my name was called. Then we were split into groups of two to summarize key points from the first chapter.

Dwight was my lab partner, and he had the unmistakable look of someone who tried too hard to make a good first impression. He reminded me a little of a golden retriever. It turns out we are in almost every class together. And he doesn't. Stop. Talking. Ever.

He walked with me to my next three classes, and my noncommittal nods and grunts of agreement did not dissuade him from continuing his running dialogue. It was white noise after a while.

Anyway, to answer one of your questions, yes, new places are tricky because I have no frame of reference. The lady in the yellow dress walking to her car with a stack of paperwork looks perfectly normal until the papers fly out of her arms and circle her body like a flock of doves. I mean, that's probably not real.

The presence of nuns and crucifixes in every room definitely makes this different from my last school. And if we pretend my ass wasn't eating my uniform shorts at every opportunity, then yes, I'd say it's been a fairly normal first couple of days. It makes me miss wearing jeans to school. Mostly because these are serious wedgies that involve discreet rectal archaeology, and it's nearly impossible to do this without being observed by someone. Luckily, I think most people ignore it because they're trying to pull their own underwear out of their crack as well.

The rest of the classes that day were a blur. If you're not going to do anything valuable during the first week, then why am I here? I wish there was some way I could tell teachers to get back to me when they're not going to waste my time. Also could've done without the get-acquainted-with-the-library bullshit.

Gym was an adventure. That was the second-to-last hour of every day this week. On the first day, Coach Russert did a timed mile run. I'm not in terrible shape or anything, but I typically don't run anywhere. Dwight tried to strike up a conversation during the whole ordeal, which was mostly annoying but a little impressive as well. I've never met anyone so committed to speaking nonstop.

"You play any sports? Basketball?" he asked. Basketball makes sense. I'm more than a head taller than all the other kids, so walking down the hall is a little bit like walking among the Munchkins in Oz.

"Nope," I said.

"This your first year at a Catholic school?"

"Yep."

"You miss your old school?" he asked.

"Nope," I said.

I wasn't trying to be an asshole. I just didn't want to vomit during the run, and one-word answers seemed safest. A couple other kids had already thrown up off to the side of the track, and one guy who wasn't paying attention slid in it and landed on his back. Some girl took out her phone and took a picture before having it confiscated. A whole summer of no physical activity definitely takes its toll.

Dwight actually wasn't the worst person to run with. He made the whole thing less painful because he kept my mind off how much I hate running. Like, really hate it. I would prefer to do almost anything else. The girl who'd rescued me earlier had already lapped us and finished her mile. It was impressive to watch her move. Even with her short little legs, she'd practically flown around the track. She disappeared a second later, but not before Dwight told me her name. Maya.

It was short and pretty. Just like her.

I ran my mile in ten minutes, thirty seconds and was grateful I wasn't last and didn't wheeze. Still, Coach looked disappointed. You can't possibly imagine how little I cared. Screw that guy. His entire job is watch us run while he does NOTHING. His disappointment is supposed to matter to me?

No, I don't think the kids at this school are actually different. Just a little richer. Obviously, there are no designer clothes to set them apart. It's the subtle accessories that do it. The guys with their designer watches and name-brand backpacks. Even their haircuts look more expensive.

With the girls, it's a little more challenging. If you know expensive shoe brands, then you can probably tell from that, but for me you can actually smell the difference. Their perfumes fluctuate from fruity nonsense to clean-smelling tonics you might find at expensive hotel spas. And none of them use them sparingly. It's like walking through a noxious cloud. It makes me want to fart just to clear the air.

And I guess they're different because they all know each other already. Even the parents seem to know each other. I say parents, but really it's just the moms. It doesn't look like any of them have jobs, so they all have time to catch up with each other. Their broods of three or four have been going to school together for years. They've been on the same soccer teams. In the same school plays. Everybody knows everybody. So I think that's mostly why it's weird. Parents just kept to themselves at my old school because none of them had time to chat in the morning. They had to shove their kids out the door and get to work.

Oh, and we have assigned seats in all our classes at this school, which I think is hilarious. At my old school, you just sat wherever you wanted. By high school they expected you to be able to control yourself, but here they like their rules. And I guess it's for good reason, since a lot of kids here like to rebel. Two girls already got sent to the nurse's office to change into longer skirts and wipe off their makeup. Get this: they were both named Mary.

Near the end of the first day, I saw Ian again. He was walking with a group of guys who, even without the uniforms, looked just like him. Well, their expressions were the same, anyway. When the bell rang, the group split and all the guys walked off toward their last class, but Ian trailed behind, watching a group of girls talking in the hallway. There was something ominous about his expression. One of the girls, a redhead with a long ponytail, maybe twelve years old, had an open backpack and a purple notebook hanging out of it.

I was the only one who saw Ian grab the notebook and toss it into a nearby trash can before turning down a hallway with a satisfied look on his face. He hadn't been grinning. He just looked like someone who'd gotten his fix. The girl, on the other hand, kept walking, completely unaware that anything had happened, so I thrust my hand into the garbage and ran the notebook over to her.

"You dropped this," I said.

"Oh, thanks!" She beamed, clearly relieved. "It has my summer assignment in it. That would've sucked."

The rest of the hallway cleared out, and when I turned to head back to my locker, I met Ian's eyes. He'd seen me fish the notebook out of the trash, and he knew that I'd seen him toss it there. It was a strange moment because I could tell by the way he was staring that he was clearly pissed that I'd caught him, but his face was impassive. It made me wonder what information he was collecting in that moment. What was he thinking about me?

I decided to help him with that by flipping him off.

A wide smile spread across his face, and he was gone again, for real this time, leaving me to wonder why anyone would do anything so deliberately mean and annoying. Just to see if he could get away with it, I guess.

Nobody aside from Assface Ian Stone has been unfriendly, but I do get a few looks every once in a while since the school is fairly small and I'm new as a junior. It's at moments like that when Rebecca normally shows up. She doesn't like me to be alone. She'll stay within my line of sight and only tries to distract me when something unpleasant creeps up. Like doubt or fear or nervous energy. That's when she'll do a cartwheel or walk on her hands or juggle fruit.

Rebecca taught me to juggle. Is that even possible? To learn to juggle from someone who's not real? Seems like that actually could have happened subconsciously by watching it on YouTube. But I remember learning from her. I remember watching the way the apples left her hands and following the movement. She was patient and showed me how to do it over and over again until I got it on my own. But I suppose I'm unreliable because I'm crazy.

Anyway, on Friday we start the religious churchy stuff.

Yeah, I've been briefed. I went to church as a little kid, and my mom has explained the main religious concepts, so I understand that the whole thing is going to be an act on my part. By now, training myself to behave a certain way no matter how I'm feeling is second nature. Church is for people who believe in things they can't see. Life for me is about seeing things I probably shouldn't believe in. So there's a nice symmetry there.

Anyway, yeah, this drug is pretty incredible. The distance from the visions is really all I needed. Just a little bit of space away from it to watch everything happen. It's not all bad stuff, actually. Sometimes it's okay. Really. I'm not complaining about all of it.

No other hallucinations to report at this point. They'll show up when they feel like it. They always do.

DOSAGE: 1 mg. Response to increased dosage is mild. Adam is cognizant of his surroundings. Hallucinations do not appear to be overwhelming at this stage. Will continue to monitor his attachment to them.

SEPTEMBER 5, 2012

I guess it doesn't really matter that I don't believe in God. Catholics are really more about attendance anyway. Every day at eleven o'clock the bells go off in the church tower, and we all have to stand and recite the prayer of Saint Augustine. In one booming, emotionless voice. Together.

Not sure I'll ever get used to that.

According to the brochure on the fridge, St. Agatha's is the oldest private school in the state, named for a woman who supposedly "refused a man's amorous advances and subsequently had her breasts cut off as penance," or something like that. Catholics celebrate weird shit.

The church itself is always featured in *Architectural*

Digest for its impressive brick facade and original four-story bell tower. And, as if this is a selling point for my attendance, the stained-glass windows were flown in from Italy in the early 1900s and blessed by Pope Leo XIII shortly before his death.

Mom and Paul had a choice of private schools in the area. The other option was an all-boys school about twenty minutes away, but my mom thought it was too "he-man." Her words, not mine. We got back from the tour, and all she said was how she couldn't get over the military look of the uniforms. Paul just shrugged. He was always going to follow her lead on this.

The funny thing is that St. Agatha's is Paul's alma mater. And even though I have no interest in religion and my mom has always been more inclined to buy healing crystals than set foot in a church, it made her feel better to send me to a school with beautiful, old brick buildings. I wasn't going to argue with her, because it doesn't matter where I go. It's just a place to be.

But it's basically like every other old church you've ever seen in your life. Half-naked angels. Uncomfortable wooden pews. And burning incense that smells like someone cooking dirty laundry. Oh, and shame. It reeks of shame.

Speaking of shame, I realize that the appealing image of a Catholic schoolgirl is cliché, but there is something distracting about the pleated skirt and vest. Within minutes of walking through the hall on Friday, I witnessed two nuns with rulers pulling girls aside and measuring the length of exposed leg from knee to skirt. Before starting school, I'd had no idea nuns still did this. It was a while before I realized I was staring and another while until I realized we were all being ushered into the church for mass. Rebecca was following me in, her lavender dress shining against the sea of navy blue and red.

She's not mad about me not talking to her anymore. Pretty sure she resented it in the beginning, when I first started taking the drug, but now she seems okay with it. If she were real, I'd point out that *she's* never spoken to me, but that's not really an argument I can win, you know? Every so often I still throw a head nod or an eye roll her way. I don't want to be a complete jerk.

On my way into the church, I felt something wet slap against the back of my neck. A spit wad. When I jumped and turned around, a severe-looking nun gave me a look that clearly wished me a painful death. Ian laughed with a couple other guys behind me, and I turned back around and kept walking even though I was pissed. I couldn't believe spit wads still happened. It occurred to me in that moment that I've never actually hit anyone before. I think I'd like to hit someone who deserves it.

Not arbitrarily, of course. I'd just really love to punch an asshole. Instant karma, you know?

It's not like I'd never been to church before. I've had all the sacraments I'm supposed to have at this point. Got all the boxes on my Catholic worksheet checked off to get into heaven, because my mom knew it would make my grandmother happy.

But it was a new place, and something in the back of my mind made me anxious. We had just increased my dosage. Remember? It's in your notes somewhere, I'm sure. But that's really something you should know off the top of your head.

I didn't tell anyone I was feeling dizzy. Not that I could've told anyone, because the only person I really talked to at school was busy being an altar boy. I think church is pretty much the only place Dwight shuts up. It was weird seeing him sitting still and not talking to the people next to him. But his robes were pretty stupid-looking, so I don't blame him for keeping quiet and just waiting for the whole thing to be over.

Anyway, we'd only gotten through the first reading, which, judging by the usual length of a Catholic mass from my memory of them as a kid, meant that the priest still had another thirty minutes of our undivided attention. Even longer if the homily was extra preachy, as they usually were. So I folded my hands and waited for the room to stop spinning.

I tried fixing my eyes on something still, but the church was full of fidgeting kids messing with their uniforms. I looked up at the stained-glass windows above the altar. They were images of the Stations of the Cross.

When we'd toured the school, they said that before Easter every class from middle school to high school would have to present their own rendition of the Stations of the Cross. They would elect one student to be Jesus, and he would be covered in fake blood and then forced to drag a heavy plywood cross across the church floor to act out each stage of his crucifixion.

This disturbed no one but me.

The stained glass *is* pretty awesome, though. Solemn and creepy at the same time. There's something soothing about the rich golds and reds when they catch the light. Even the blood on Jesus's face seems less threatening in glass. But after a few minutes, I knew something was wrong.

Jesus's chest had begun to rise and fall. I looked away from him and forced my eyes to the sixth station. It's the one where a woman named Veronica steps out of the crowd to wipe sweat and blood off Jesus's face as he's being marched to his death. It's my favorite one, easily the kindest of the stations. But after I stared at her for a second, she began to breathe, and her colorful clothes turned black as she turned her face to me. Slowly, all the figures in the stained glass turned their faces to me.

Even the angels gazed down at me, their glassy faces half reflected in the morning light. A strange wind rustled their wings, and I closed my eyes and bowed my head, hoping the kids sitting next to me would think I was praying. The angels were all watching me from the glass, and I knew that if I stared back I might not be able to look away again.

That was when I felt Rebecca's eyes on my back. When I turned around, she smiled at me. That worried smile she always wears when she knows something is wrong but doesn't want to make a big deal. I knew it wasn't real. Hell, I knew *she* wasn't real, but it was hard to convince myself in the moment. I just tried to let the communion procession distract me.

I didn't get up for communion. You know, where they hand out pieces of Jesus made of stale wafers.

It's funny how people still seem surprised when you don't get communion. When I was little, my mom explained that it usually meant someone thought they were too filled with sin to receive Jesus. Even if I hadn't been feeling weird, I just don't like the idea of some old guy shoving food in my mouth. Or sharing a wineglass with a hundred strangers. It's the grossest thing I've ever seen. They pass the same glass to everyone, wipe it, turn it, and then pass it off to the next person. Like wiping it with the same white cloth over and over magically makes it clean. *The Blood of Christ . . . and the spit from that girl with the questionable cold sore.*

Soon, Rebecca was sitting at the edge of the row, two pews in front of me, running her fingers through her hair, looking concerned. I wanted to reassure her, but then everyone would have seen me talking to nothing. Still, it's not her fault she's not real.

Instead, I hunched my shoulders and took a few deep breaths, trying to keep my head from spinning.

"Are you okay?" the girl next to me whispered. It took a second for me to register that it was Maya and then another second to tell her it was just a headache, which wasn't a complete lie. I say that a lot to people. And it bothered me that I couldn't remember if she'd always been sitting next to me or if she'd just moved to that spot.

Without another word, she got up from her seat, walked to the edge of the pew, and disappeared out of sight toward the back of the church. A minute later she was back with a bottle of water. She handed it to me.

I was glad she didn't come back with aspirin. Not sure how I would have told her that it might interfere with what I was already taking.

Because I hallucinate and hear voices.

"Drink," she said. "Sometimes it helps."

"Thanks," I whispered back. "I'm Adam."

"Maya," she said, turning her attention back to the altar. Dwight had already told me this, of course, but I accepted it as new information and then tried to stare at her using only my peripheral vision. Dwight had told me her last name was Salvador, and I'm pretty sure she's Filipino. Her short brown hair brushed the top of her shoulders in perfect even strokes. I was impressed that she'd managed to make it all the way down our pew and back without incurring the wrath of the nun at the end of the row. Nuns were usually quick to punish any disturbance during mass, but in this case Maya had moved with such swift determination that they couldn't possibly object. Sister Catherine nodded in her direction.

I never would have gotten away with that.

Maya paid attention to what the priest was saying. I could see the force of concentration in her eyes, but every so often I felt her gaze drift toward me.

It took a minute for me to realize that she was checking to make sure I was okay.

I pretended that this didn't matter to me.

I'd had friends back at my old school. I'd grown up with them. Ridden bikes with them. Snuck out after curfew with them. But when they found out what I was, they were afraid of me, just like Paul. After the incident at school and all the strange behavior, they stopped calling.

I'd known Michael and Kevin since we were five. We'd been on the same T-ball team together. They'd at least sent "Get Well Soon" cards when I left school, no doubt forced into it by their mothers, but no one came around after that. My best friend, Todd, disappeared completely.

Get Well Soon.

Like crazy is something you can sleep off.

But I know they were afraid and I get that. I'm not angry with them or anything.

I felt a nudge on my arm and looked down to see Maya staring up at me again.

"I'm fine," I said quietly. She looked at me appraisingly and then turned back, clearly not convinced that I wasn't lying.

The angels in the stained-glass window were still watching me, but I wasn't paying attention.

Rebecca skipped ahead of me and turned back to smile in Maya's direction.

After mass, all three hundred of us walked back across the lawn to our classes. Mine was religious theory, taught by Sister Catherine. It is the one class I don't have with Dwight but do have with Maya. Sister Catherine is the youngest teacher at the school, but easily the toughest bride of Christ I've ever met. She'd probably bust out a ruler if she could, but when she's angry about something, she wrinkles her forehead and her white-blond eyebrows practically disappear.

"Today," she said, "I'm going to see how well you read your assignment." She held up a red prayer book that had arrived in the mail about a month before school started. Part of our summer homework had been to read all the prayers, but Sister Catherine's mouth was twisted in a maniacal grin. "I would like for you to write out the mysteries of the rosary, the Prayer of Saint Augustine, and Hail, Holy Queen from memory," she said.

Everyone in the room groaned. It had not been part of the assignment to memorize the prayers, which is probably why Maya also had an irritated expression on her face. She tightened her lips and wrinkled her nose in distaste. Even a die-hard Catholic would probably not have the rosaries memorized, but if she'd known it was a challenge in advance, she would have memorized them all. I could just tell she was that kind of person.

"This isn't for credit," Sister Catherine added. "But if you write them *all* down correctly, you will have no religion homework for the rest of the year. You have one hour." Her smile was victorious but mostly repulsive.

I'm actually really good at memorizing things. That's one of the skills my little problem hasn't taken away.

Sometimes people with my condition have a rough time organizing their thoughts, but storing information has never been an issue for me. Over the summer, it took me maybe an hour to etch the whole thing onto the wall of my brain, so it took less than fifteen minutes to regurgitate it back onto paper. Maya raised an eyebrow in my direction when I finished way before anyone else, but she turned her head back to her own paper pretty quickly and, from the look of it, tried to make up something that sounded like a prayer she'd read.

I'm not usually into prayers, but there is a line in Hail, Holy Queen that I enjoyed.

To thee do we cry, poor banished children of Eve.

It's supposed to sound devastating. *Banished children of Eve.*

But it actually sounds whiny. Like getting in trouble with your dad so you go running to your mom.

To thee do we cry.

I dropped off my paper at the end of class and stepped out into the hall feeling relieved that I at least wouldn't have religion homework to worry about. I watched Maya navigate her way through the crowd and smiled at the way she managed to avoid touching anyone. Her shiny brown hair reminded me of hot chocolate the way it seemed to flow over the top of her shoulders. I watched her a lot longer than I should have.

Rebecca was sitting on top of a row of lockers, holding her knees against her chest and smiling to herself. She had a goofy expression of longing on her face that bugged me for some reason.

Dwight and I eat lunch together every day. Not sure if it was a conscious choice on my part, but I don't mind admitting that it is probably the best thing about him—having someone to eat lunch with. It's really awkward eating alone or trying to find a place to eat when all the tables are full. That is one of those moments when you shouldn't feel bad that no one is going out of their way to make room for you, but you kind of do anyway.

Maya eats with a few girls toward the back of the room. Far away from the überrich kids in the middle of the lunch tables. Today she looked over at me and I looked away, pretending that I hadn't just been staring at her. It wasn't convincing.

So anyway, Dwight and I sit together. Sometimes I talk, but mostly he does. I know more about him than I ever expected to know, actually. Like how he's been an altar boy since middle school. And a vegan since he was nine because he saw a chicken beheaded on his great-aunt's farm. And a Columbian Squire since his mom filled out the form and made him start going to meetings with his grandfather. If you don't know, the Knights of

Columbus is a Catholic organization made up of wrinkly old men and their sons who raise money for charities and sometimes political campaigns that focus on Catholic values, like having as many kids as humanly possible and not eating meat on Fridays during Lent. Ian and a lot of the guys in my classes were Squires. Dwight got roped into it early, but it doesn't seem to bother him.

He doesn't mind when I don't talk, which is nice, especially when I see something weird and I'm trying to concentrate on not seeing it.

Like today, when the mobsters in pin-striped suits showed up in the cafeteria. I winced when the gunshots went off, but the drug held up nicely.

"Are you okay?" Dwight asked.

"Yeah, fine," I told him. "Headache."

I watched as the last mobster's body fell to the ground, draining blood all over the clean linoleum floor. The mobsters had even twitched a little when they died, for cinematic effect. I looked into their pale dead faces for a second. They looked like extras from *The Godfather.* The mob boss stared directly at me before slipping out the door and vanishing into a sea of uniforms.

My hallucinations are a familiar cast of characters. I've seen the mobsters before, but this was the first time I've kept my seat when the guns went off.

Progress.

DOSAGE: 1 mg. Same dosage. Appears more antagonistic than in previous sessions.

SEPTEMBER 12, 2012

"So tell me about your father?"

Well, shit. That didn't take long. Only four weeks in and we've already diagnosed the cause of all my problems. The epicenter of my delirium. The real reason I am the way I am.

My daddy done left me.

That's what you want me to say, isn't it? That I'm emotionally scarred because my dad didn't want to stick around to be my dad? Or that I blame my disease on him? That would be easy.

You can't blame a disease on someone. Even if I wanted to. That's the stupidest thing I've ever heard. Do you really think I'm so much of a loser that I need someone to blame? Anyway, the disease is from my mom's side.

My dad is just an asshole. This is an undeniable truth. He left when I was eight.

When he didn't come home for dinner one night, my mom told me he wasn't coming back. I remember how she'd looked when she said it. Like all the blood had been drained from her face. She didn't cry. She just looked tired.

That's why my dad is an asshole.

My mom was *always* tired. Every day she got home from work, she was exhausted. And he never tried to make it any easier for her. It's better that he left because he couldn't be what we needed anyway. No, not *couldn't*. Wouldn't.

I'm not sure where he went right after he left. If Mom knew, she never said. And I didn't ask.

A few years after he left, I got a letter from him. I was eleven and I used to grab the mail before my mom got home. The return address was somewhere in Barstow, California. I tore it up after I read it, but I remember what it said.

Dear Adam,

I've started this letter to you so many times and haven't had the strength to send it. Your mom was always the good one. The one who knows what to do in any situation. She makes problems disappear

*like magic. That's who she is and that's why I fell
in love with her.*

*But me, I'm the problem and I couldn't keep
breaking her heart while she waited for me to be
the man she needed.*

*As for you, I think you're better off without me.
And I want you to have the best chance for success.
I owe you that at least.*

Dad

Not "Love, Dad."

I didn't write back or tell my mom about the letter he
didn't have the "strength" to send for three years. How
much *strength* does writing a goddamned letter take, anyway? And it was 106 words. I counted. That really wore
you out, didn't it, Dad?

At least he was honest. He knew he was a coward. He
knew my mom deserved better.

But the truth was that he didn't really love us. When
you love somebody, you try to be better.

So I don't miss him.

6

DOSAGE: 1.5 mg. Increase in dosage appears to be showing positive results. Subject notes an increase in the appearance of hallucinations, but reaction to hallucinations remains minimal. Excellent progress.

SEPTEMBER 19, 2012

This relationship is weird because you already know that my doctors increased my ToZaPrex dosage. You already know that there are side effects, and because you are a Harvard-educated psychologist, you know what those side effects are.

But I'm in a good mood and the drug is working well, so I'll tell you about "my experience" with the increase.

The headaches come and go. Mostly when I'm in crowded places where there is a lot of movement. And there's some sensitivity to light. And increased hallucinations.

Rest assured, I'm very aware of what is real and what

is not. I don't have those moments of panic I used to, like when I wasn't sure if my bed was actually on fire. But I see stuff I shouldn't everywhere. There's the man in the suit with the big metal briefcase that always spills open, flinging money everywhere. And the woman with the huge dog dragging her across the lawn. Then there's the weird shadowy guy who hangs out at the edge of my line of sight, always dashing into an alleyway. The mobsters. Rebecca. A few others I only see once in a while.

With a last name like Petrazelli, I guess it makes sense to you that I would see mobsters. They are practically required images for all Italian male schizophrenics, right? I'm not sure if my mobster hallucinations are due to my heritage or to the fact that my mom was obsessed with the *Godfather* movies.

Don't tell her that. I'd hate for her to blame herself for any of my crazy.

But yeah, I guess the hallucinations are all symbolic of something. The mobsters, for example, can't be reasoned with. The henchmen carry out the orders of a shadowy don who never has to get his hands dirty. My neighborhood is as far away from the Italian Mafia as the moon, yet when I see them, they don't feel foreign. They feel like they fit in. They're like the weasels in *Who Framed Roger Rabbit*, annoying little henchmen who say things like "yeah, boss" in a loud, nasally voice.

Every now and then, I'll get a different hallucination, something that I haven't seen before, and that's when I have to be careful, because there's a small chance that they are not a hallucination at all—just a new person I've never seen before. So I wait for the signs. The strange eye color. The weird voice. The fact that no one else can see them when they do something odd. That's actually the only reason I knew that the old lady in the track-suit running down our street was a hallucination. She did backflips in our driveway. The couple pushing their stroller across the street didn't even look up, and I'm almost positive they were real.

I'm not sure if this is a side effect of the drug, so I'll tell you what happened, and you can tell me.

St. Agatha's has a pool. Boys and girls aren't allowed to use it at the same time because swimsuits are provocative and inspire horny teenagers to have impure thoughts. I'd like to tell them that these thoughts would exist regardless of the swimsuits, but whatever. This week we were split into groups and told to swim laps.

I didn't think it was possible to hate anything more than running, but I will say this: I actually *am* a lot more motivated to keep swimming since the alternative is drowning at the bottom of a pool that everybody probably pees in.

I popped my head out of the water just long enough to see Ian swimming a few lanes over from me. I hate to admit it, but he is an excellent swimmer. He finished his laps before anyone else and spent the rest of the class sitting on the edge of the pool, watching everyone with a superior look on his face. He wrinkled his nose in Dwight's direction, emphasizing his usual arrogant glance. Granted, Dwight was swimming as awkwardly as humanly possible and was the only one in the water wearing nose plugs and bright blue goggles. But I bet Ian would have looked at him like that anyway.

So here's the part I need your help with. I get that my hallucinations aren't the most trustworthy people, but sometimes I feel like they're trying to tell me something I can't see on my own. Does that even make sense?

I was the last one in the locker room, and I'd just finished getting dressed when I heard a splash. Rebecca, who had been sitting cross-legged on a bench waiting for me to leave, bolted out of the room. I don't mean that she was running in a circle or darting between lockers toward the door. She actually took off sprinting toward the pool, and since this had never happened before, I followed her.

The pool was empty except for one thrashing body tangled in the floating swimming lanes. I didn't have my specs on, but whoever it was, they clearly couldn't swim.

So I jumped in. I figured if it turned out that this wasn't real, the worst that could happen was I got wet.

Trying to save someone from drowning is not as glamorous as it sounds. Once I'd gotten close enough to actually help them, I was rewarded with a swift kick in the face by someone desperately struggling to stay afloat.

"Stop moving!" I yelled.

"Why? So I can drown faster?" It was Maya.

"No," I panted, tasting the blood that was now dripping from my nose. "So I can grab you and pull you to the side."

She was hesitant to leave the safety of the swim lanes, but eventually I managed to pull her off and swim us both to the ladder on the edge of the pool. She climbed out and threw up over the drain.

"You can't swim?" I asked, taking deep breaths. She glared at me for stating the obvious. "Okay," I said. "Any reason you were in here to begin with?"

She pointed at the stack of clipboards near the door. "Coach Russert asked me to come get them since I'd be passing the athletics office on my way to English," she said.

"And you decided to go for a swim?" I asked. My nose was bleeding pretty heavily at this point, but she continued to glare at me.

She pointed at a fallen tower of safety vests and breathed, "I tripped."

It got awkward pretty quickly after that. We both realized at exactly the same time that we were both soaking wet lying on the floor of the pool room, next to a puddle of Maya's vomit, while blood poured steadily out of my nose. The good thing is I think the awkwardness softened her.

"I'm sorry about that," she said, pointing at my face.

"It's okay," I said. Actually, it was not okay. It hurt like hell, but I wasn't about to tell her that.

We both stood up and shuffled in place for a minute. In the movies when this sort of thing happens, it's usually followed by a dramatic love scene or, at the very least, an undying pledge of friendship. But we both just stared at each other until finally she said, "Thanks for saving my life," which is a lot less dramatic when someone actually says it than Disney would have you believe.

"You're welcome," I said. For a split second, I saw her smile and the effect was stunning. I didn't get to enjoy it, though. She bolted through the door to the girls' locker room, leaving me there to wonder what the hell just happened.

Did I run to the sound of the splash when she fell in? Or did I follow Rebecca when she ran?

Does that even matter?

* * *

My first confession at St. Agatha's was this past Friday after mass. All the grades take turns going, which still amazes me because of how much time the whole process takes. It's like an hour and forty-five minutes of waiting for your turn. Five minutes with the priest and then five minutes kneeling afterward. That's a lot of time that probably could be spent learning stuff.

I'd grown up Catholic, but I'd only ever gone once before, when I was about eight years old, because that's the age kids typically are for their first confession. Needless to say, there had been nothing to confess. Eight-year-olds don't get up to much. But I felt guilty, so I told the priest some stuff I felt guilty about, and he seemed satisfied with that.

I can't understand why anyone would feel compelled to tell a complete stranger all their sins (as I sit here and tell you all my problems). More importantly, I don't believe for a second that anyone actually does it.

You just make up a bunch of stuff while you wait in line.

This makes me wonder about how other people feel guilt. Because I think I'm doing it wrong. I don't generally feel guilty about the things I do—I feel guilty for NOT feeling guilty about the things I do. Like yesterday. I had a full internal monologue about how I would give away my schizophrenia if I could. I thought about choosing someone who deserved it and how great I would feel after I gave it to them, knowing that it didn't belong to me anymore.

I would feel the most wonderful sense of relief, and for a brief second I would be happy to think that I could cast my problems off on someone else. Then I would feel guilty for not feeling guilty about it. Because that pretty much makes me an awful person, right?

I looked around at all the faces waiting to go into confession. They were bored.

Maya sat in the pews on the other side of the aisle and smiled at me, then rolled her eyes a little as if to say, *This is stupid.* I made the same face back. *Yeah, I know, right?* But I don't actually know what my expression looked like, so maybe she didn't get that from the look. Maybe the look actually conveyed nothing. It was the first time I'd seen her since I'd pulled her out of the pool, but for some reason, it didn't feel awkward.

The choir was practicing for Sunday mass, and I cringed when they started to sing. I've discovered that it's pretty easy to let information wash over me if I want it to or if it's boring, unless someone puts it in a church song. Then that shit is stuck in my head for life.

When it was my turn, I walked into the confessional

and knelt behind the mesh screen. I said what you're supposed to say. "Bless me, Father, for I have sinned. It has been eight years since my last confession."

"Why so long, my son?" He was a fill-in priest with an Irish accent who says mass for Father Benjamin sometimes. I hate when people say "my son" to people who are not their son. It's creepy. But he is legitimately Irish, which makes him slightly more interesting than the average American priest. Kind of like a leprechaun who grants wishes. I imagined him saying, *They're always after me Lucky Charms,* and tried to feel guilty about it. But I didn't. That shit is hilarious.

"I think telling someone your sins is a waste of time." I could hear him shift a little in his chair. It might have been rude to say that, but it was probably worse to lie in confession.

"A waste of time?" he asked.

"Yes," I said. Then I added, "Sorry."

I waited for Father Patrick to reach his hands through the screen to strangle me, but nothing happened. The silence built for a while until I felt compelled to speak. "Did I give you a heart attack?"

I was glad when he laughed and said, "No."

"Do people usually just come in, tell you their sins, and go on their merry way?"

"Usually," he said. I could tell he was still smiling.

"But once in a while I get a kid like you who wants to know the point of all this."

"And what do you tell them?" I asked.

"That telling someone your sins ... *actually* telling someone your sins is like admitting you are flawed."

"You think we don't know we're flawed? Why does that need to be rubbed in our faces all the time?"

He was quiet for a while. Then he said, "Would you accept it if I told you that it's just another way to communicate with God?"

"And if I don't believe in God?" He shifted in his seat again. Probably because that threatens his job security.

"Then use the time to think about the kind of person you want to be. And at the very least," he said quietly, "believe in yourself."

Not what I'd expected to hear from him, but I still got the hell out of there before he could assign me any prayers.

After his fairly logical assessment, I would have felt compelled to say them.

When I walked out of the confessional, Sister Catherine pointed toward the pew to her left and pressed her fingers to her lips, like I was five years old and didn't know not to whistle or shriek with glee as I skipped down the aisle. Maya was sitting directly across from me now, praying. Presumably.

When I knelt down in my row, I bowed my head the way you're supposed to and closed my eyes. A second later, I felt someone sit down next to me.

"Hey," Maya whispered.

"Hey," I whispered back. "Aren't you going to get in trouble for talking in church?"

"Not if you stare straight ahead and keep your voice down," she said calmly. "Sometimes the Holy Spirit commands you to pray out loud." She rolled her eyes and smiled. "How's your nose?"

"Not bad," I lied. I wasn't going to tell her that it still hurt, especially when she looked guilty about it. Luckily, it wasn't bruised, just sore.

"Listen, Sister Catherine is going to ask you to be on Academic Team. I overheard her telling another teacher after class about how you memorized all those prayers."

"That loser group that does decathlon tournaments?"

"That's us," she said, raising an eyebrow. I think at that point I made a lame attempt to apologize for calling her a loser.

"Please," she said, ignoring me. "We've embraced it. Plus you have to have an extracurricular here. If you don't play an instrument or a sport, it's Academic Team."

"So I don't have a choice, actually."

"Well, you're tall. Do you play basketball?"

I laughed and then abruptly turned it into a cough

when Sister Catherine looked my way. I'd been recruited once to try out for the team at my old school, but I have no coordination. I can barely put my spectacles on without poking myself in the eye. It took less than ten minutes for the team to realize that I was basically useless unless they needed someone to hold the hoop.

"I'll get your number from you later so I can text you the meeting spot for practice," she said.

"Just give me yours," I whispered.

"I don't have a pen or anything," she said.

"I'll remember."

"Of course you will," she smirked. I tried not to look pleased with myself when she told me her number and I memorized it.

Sister Catherine *did* ask me to join the team later that day. Since I had no religion homework to worry about, I could use that time to memorize facts, she said. *Awesome.*

Meanwhile, Rebecca was doing pirouettes at the front of the classroom, her blond hair swaying like spun gold while a choir of voices sang "Amazing Grace." It distracted me for a minute until I saw Sister Catherine's eyes flicker to mine. I thought I'd covered it up pretty well, but she'd noticed. There was a moment of understanding between us but also a warning that I had been obvious. I took a deep breath and focused all my attention to the front of the room until the end of class.

I sent Maya a text later that day. It took me ten minutes to write it, and all it said was "Hey, this is Adam."

A second later, she responded with "Thx."

When Paul picked me up after school, he didn't say much, but he drove through McDonald's for shakes. He's still afraid of me. But it feels like he doesn't want to be.

My pocket buzzed when we were pulling into the driveway, and I saw that Maya had sent me another text.

"Welcome to the loser group, by the way."

I think she likes me.

DOSAGE: 1.5 mg. Same dosage. Adam appears to be opening up about his illness. Some increased hostility regarding therapy. Still refuses to communicate verbally.

SEPTEMBER 26, 2012

Your comments about my diary seeming "too self-aware" to be authentic are bullshit. This is just me. You're just pissed that I won't talk to you.

It's actually kind of annoying to be quizzed by your therapist. You asking me what I know about schizophrenia is like me asking you what you know about dressing like an arrogant snob. I know it because I live it.

Here are the facts, which you already know, but I'll tell you anyway because I want to appear clever and I'm desperately seeking your approval. *Obviously.*

"Schizophrenia" is a Greek word that literally translates to "schizein" (to split) and "phren" (mind). But it doesn't mean split personality. And it doesn't mean multiple personalities. The "split" refers to a rift between mental functions.

It is a cornucopia of shit, basically. Which you already know.

Never goes away. Never gets normal. And never lets you relax.

Side note: Your jacket is stupid. You shouldn't wear plaid. Also, I hate your hair. Is that mousse that you're using to make it so wavy? Knock it off. And your fly was unzipped for the entire hour of our last session, but I didn't say anything because (1) I didn't want you to think I was staring at your junk, and (2) I don't talk to you, and that would have been really difficult to mime.

Here's something you don't know. My great-uncle Greg had it. He was my grandmother's brother, and the thing I remember most about their relationship was that my grandma liked to pretend he was normal. She never made it sound like he was anything other than a normal man with problems. I never even heard the word "schizophrenia" mentioned when anybody talked about him. I'm not sure that was helpful, but it was a different time and people had less sympathy for diseases that weren't killing anybody. Plus my mom said Uncle Greg was never diagnosed. If he hadn't had a family, he probably would've died on the streets.

I liked him. He was soft-spoken. Never complained. There wasn't a mean bone in his body. He was the kind of guy who hid money in library books when he returned them and always let people go in front of him in line at the grocery store. And he played the piano better than anyone I'd ever heard. He taught himself and could pretty much play by ear.

Since he lived with my grandma for most of his life and had no real expenses, he taught piano to kids who couldn't afford lessons. Sometimes they would pay him in vegetables from their gardens. Sometimes their moms baked cookies. Once, he came home with a scarf one of his students had knitted for him, and he wore it every day for a month. In July.

But the point is, if they wanted to learn, they left knowing how to play.

I really wish I'd wanted to learn back then.

He died around the time my dad left, but I'll never forget the thing he said to me when he was trying to teach me how to play. He'd overheard my mom telling my grandma about me getting teased at school for something stupid. This was way before they knew anything was wrong with me.

"Most people are afraid of themselves, Adam. They carry that fear everywhere hoping no one will notice." Before I could ask him what that had to do with anything, he laughed. He had a ridiculous laugh, like a horn that sort of exploded out of him at odd moments. My mom said it was a big hit when I was a baby.

Even though he was never diagnosed, I know he was like me. The difference is that he was really kind, and it doesn't matter how crazy you are if you're a genuinely nice person. People will forgive you.

You asked me once what I was afraid of. I didn't answer because I didn't feel like it. Talking about it makes me sound lame. But it's late and I can't sleep. And the thing that creeps into my mind when I can't sleep is here.

You've probably noticed by now that I'm capable of defending myself against anything that might actually stumble into my room in the middle of the night, but my fists are still clenched and my eyes are still searching for the source of the scratching noise beneath my floor-boards because there is a part of me that still believes that what I see and hear *is real*. That something is trying to get me.

I remember a story I read once about a man who thought the people on his train were trying to kill him. He'd convinced himself that they could read his thoughts and were going to drag him off the train at the next stop and bludgeon him to death.

He locked himself in the bathroom for over an hour.

When the train finally reached the next stop, he ran screaming from the compartment before leaping for the station platform, missing it, and cracking his head open on the snowy bank below.

He was thirty-seven. Pretty young to die.

I find that with most stories, at least the ones I've read in school, trains nearly always mean something. They are adventure or death.

In the corner of my room, I see a man standing in shadow. He's wearing a black bowler hat and carrying a cane with a curved handle. Every few minutes, he checks his watch and looks at me.

"It's almost time," he keeps saying under his breath. "Get ready to run. Train's coming."

"Almost time for what?" I want to ask him.

But he just smiles and says nothing. He doesn't have to.

And even though he's creepy and I wish he'd leave, *he* isn't what I'm afraid of.

I'm afraid of the way things used to be when I believed he was real.

I'm afraid that someday I won't be able to watch the parade of hallucinations without doing what they tell me to do because I'm afraid the drug will stop working. And everyone might have good reason to be afraid of me.

8

DOSAGE: 1.5 mg. Same dosage. No change.

OCTOBER 3, 2012

The naked guy visits once in a while. He's probably the weirdest hallucination I have. Taller than me. And stark naked. Cheeks to the wind. In my head I call him Jason. No reason, he just looks like a Jason.

He's actually a pretty nice guy. He reminds me to hold doors open. To say thank you. That kind of stuff. But we don't have a relationship beyond that. Jason is just a giant, naked presence wandering the halls in my school. So that's crazy even for a hallucination.

I'm not supposed to call myself crazy anymore. It was in one of those books my mom bought after I was diagnosed. They all talk about loving your freak-show kid no matter how many imaginary friends he's got.

So anyway, Jason-the-naked and I were sitting outside homeroom when Ian walked by with one other guy carrying a bucket marked *WASTE* from the biology lab. They were clearly on their way to dispose of the chunky leftovers they couldn't pour down the sink, and I didn't look up until two seconds before they passed. I didn't even have time to register what had happened when they sloshed a third of the stuff into my lap and took off running down the corridor like idiots with what was left dripping all over the floor. I could still hear their laughter ringing in my ears. They'd deliberately poured that shit all over me. Even Jason, the nicest guy I know, who makes excuses for everyone, could only say, "Dude, that's messed up," before disappearing completely.

Trying to get cleaned up in the bathroom proved useless, so I walked to the nurse's office. After looking at me like I'd doused myself with frog guts and formaldehyde on purpose, the nurse handed me some "loaner" uniform shorts that fit around the waist but were at least two inches too short. A woman with long, curly black hair stifled a laugh when I walked out of the bathroom.

"Sorry," she said, still smiling. "There's nothing longer."

"Awesome."

"Only two more hours to go, though. Don't worry."

I like how people only tell you not to worry about stuff when it's something they don't care about. The new shorts did not entirely remove the faint smell of science drifting off my pants, and since my underwear had been soaked through, I took the opportunity to ditch them in the trash when I changed.

I had an hour of English class to sit through before gym. Dwight had seen me walking to the nurse's office, so I told him what happened. He kept up a stream of commentary throughout class about Ian being a jerk, which I appreciated despite the fact that if I moved the wrong way I could hear the squelching sound of moisture between my butt cheeks.

Going commando at school is weird.

Going commando during gym is wildly uncomfortable.

The mesh net in my running shorts didn't help much. I could feel my balls chafing against the elastic. Ian and the other guy from earlier (I think his name is Zane? Or Blane? Or something equally obnoxious) turned around to look at me a few times during class with faces that were just asking to be smooshed into the ground. Rebecca shook her head at me from the bleachers.

I walked with Maya back to our lockers afterward. Dwight had raced back to church for an altar boy meeting, so this was one of the few times since saving her life that we were actually alone together. She sniffed the air curiously for a few seconds but didn't say anything. What was originally a faint chemical odor had become a faint chemical odor with a hint of sweaty balls.

"I think Ian is jealous that you're taller than he is."

"What?" I asked. The comment was so completely out of nowhere.

"You're tall. He's average height, and his brothers are all really tall. I think he's messing with you because he's jealous."

"Why would anyone mess with someone because they're tall?"

"Well, you're also better-looking than he is," she said.

"Oh," I said.

"See you later."

She turned a corner before I could think of anything clever to say, and as a result, I spent the rest of the day feeling like an idiot. Oh.

I said "Oh"?!?

I could have said almost anything else. Like *Thank you*. Oh.

My level of stupidity has reached epic proportions. Even now, I have no idea what I should have said.

I'm not supposed to think of my disease as something to deal with. I'm told it's better to think of it as a piece of me that does not communicate well with the rest of me. But that's bullshit.

The important thing about being crazy is knowing that you're crazy. The *knowing* part makes you less crazy.

I wonder if you've ever had a patient who refused to speak to you before. This must be the easiest money you've ever made. To read my notes, nod smugly for a while, and try to engage me in conversation.

Do you feel guilty taking money from people with mental illnesses? I guess you don't actually, just their families. The people who trust you to make them better. Kind of like people who waste all their money on psychics who tell them what they want to hear.

Still, but I don't blame you for choosing your line of work. People with mental problems are fascinating. Once, when I was ten, Paul and my mom took me to San Francisco, which, it turns out, is filled with homeless people. So, a lot of crazies.

It's hard not to stare when they're having a moment. This one guy in the park had managed to blow bubbles by mixing his spit with a little bit of soap. He was sitting on a trash can lid, blowing spit bubbles at everyone who passed him, having a wild conversation with someone none of us could see.

I remember laughing at the time and my mom giving me the most severe look I'd ever seen. I don't think I'd laugh now. Well, maybe. That shit is still pretty funny.

I don't waste time feeling sorry for people with mental problems, because I don't want people to waste time feeling sorry for me. I don't need the pity—it doesn't do anyone any good. We see the world differently and make up our own rules. That's what terrifies everyone. Maybe they're jealous. But probably not.

That's why I like reading about the saints. They ban a lot of books at St. Agatha's (like the Harry Potter ones because they supposedly lead children to believe in the occult), but they have endless volumes of saint biographies, which are actually more scandalous. It's nice to read about people who were batshit crazy and got away with it.

And you know who's really insane? But also awesome?

Joan of Arc. The Maid of Orléans.

She had visions of the Archangel Michael, Saint Catherine, and Saint Margaret, all instructing her to support Charles VII and recover France from British rule during the Hundred Years' War. She heard voices and actually led an army in the siege of Orléans. People were so willing to accept religious miracles that they let a teenager lead a political movement because she was divinely inspired. She was a radiant vision of power and defiance.

And so of course they burned her.

Maya sent me a text yesterday with the date and time of the first Academic Team practice. So I responded:

Me: Thanks. Anything I should know before first practice?

Maya: Everything. Miscellaneous facts. Old movies. Country capitals. Classic literature.

Me: What kind of old movies?

Maya: Like Gone with the Wind. Wizard of Oz. Casablanca. They like black and white stuff.

Me: Cool. I've seen Casablanca.

Maya: Congratulations

Me: ☺

*Note: A smiley face is an appropriate response to almost anything when you don't know how else to reply.

9

DOSAGE: 1.5 mg. Same dosage, definite improvement. Visibly more relaxed in session.

OCTOBER 10, 2012

I made pad Thai with chicken a few nights ago, completely from scratch. It's probably the best thing I've ever made, so yeah, that's what I'm most proud of. I like feeding people. It's an easy way to make them happy, and I get a rush from the instant gratification.

I'm really more of a baker, but it used to make my mom happy when dinner was already made when she got home. Paul can barely make toast on his own, so it was up to me. It's kind of refreshing that there's one thing he can't do.

No, I'm not self-conscious about liking to bake. Yes, I've definitely been teased about it before, but screw them. They can't feed themselves and I can. That's powerful. It's really the only truly powerful thing about me. I might not always have a handle on my life, but if I'm hungry, I have more options than grilled cheese and cereal. And if I ever need to cook for anyone else, I can do it. There's something liberating about being able to make food. No one will ever have to slave over a hot stove for me. I have that at least.

I also don't experience as many symptoms when I'm cooking. It takes too much of my concentration. It's a precise art. Okay, you can take a few liberties with herbs and spices, but every detail can be replicated with the right amount of practice.

The other night, when I went to make breaded chicken, I noticed that someone had hidden all the knives. When I asked my mom about it, she hesitated before telling me that Paul thought it was a good idea for someone to be home if I was going to be cooking. She didn't look me in the eye, which made me think about the conversation they must have had about getting rid of dangerous stuff. It was kind of out of character for Paul. He has a reason for everything he does. I have no idea what might've spooked him.

It was pretty crappy of them. I mean they could've just told me. I would've understood. I don't want them to be afraid of me. They didn't have to hide everything so I looked like some unbalanced psychopath. It's not like

I'm going to stop cutting the chicken and go after people because I'm feeling "stabby."

I mean, it's unlikely.

Right?

Maya saw my notebook. The one I keep my recipes in. When she asked me about it, I just shrugged and told her I like to cook.

"Cook what?" she asked.

"Everything." I told her about my mom and how she always worked late, but no matter how tired she was she still dragged me to the kitchen table to talk about my day over a meal. Even if it was only cereal. She thought that was important. Sharing a meal with someone. And ever since then, I've thought that the meal should matter. It should mean something.

Which is funny because Mom is a pretty average cook. I don't mean that she's bad or anything. In fact, most of the stuff she makes is tasty. She just doesn't love cooking, and you can always taste that in the food.

Country-style biscuits are the only things she makes with absolute love. Big, fluffy, butter-filled lumps of cheesy goodness. They're the first things I learned how to bake, and they're the only things my mom still makes better.

I guess I'd been talking for a while, because when I looked up, Maya had taken off her glasses. She was different without them. I hadn't noticed the tiny flecks of green in her eyes until then. Then I realized I was staring at her.

"So that was a lot of personal, warm, fuzzy information that you probably didn't need," I said. She handed back my notebook and smiled.

"My mom can't stand cooking," she said. "She's always hated it. There are three of us kids, me and my little brothers. Plus my dad. When she gets home from the hospital, she doesn't even want to look at the kitchen. Dinner is basically whatever I feel like making. So a lot of scrambled eggs at our house." She looked tired for a moment.

"My dad doesn't make a regular paycheck," she told me matter-of-factly. "He's a freelance plumber. And he makes decent money when work is stable, but when it's not, my mom takes on extra shifts and he stays home with the boys." She looked at me again. "They weren't ready for twins."

"I don't think anyone is ready for that. That's like one hundred percent more baby," I said.

"And so much poop. The diapers were unreal." She shuddered and I laughed.

She didn't say any more on the subject, so I had to fill

in the blanks myself. Two kids when you are only expecting one makes for more work and costs more money. Maya didn't say it like her mom felt as if she had been dealt a low blow. She'd accepted it and moved on. And the fact that her dad was there with her brothers was a good thing.

You asked me to describe Maya. Did you mean physically? Seems kind of pervy for you to ask me to tell you what she looks like in excruciating detail.

She's tiny.

I've said that before, but I'm not sure you understand. People have called me Sasquatch and Frankenstein my whole life, and when Maya sits next to me, I actually look the part. Seriously. Torch-wielding villagers would come to her aid if they saw us together.

She's got huge eyes, like an innocent woodland creature's, and small hands that always move when she talks.

Personality-wise, I probably should also mention that Maya isn't exactly friendly. From my limited experience so far, it's absolutely clear that she doesn't like people in general. I mean, she's kind and everything—but she has a finite circle of people who she actually cares about. If she chooses you, it's kind of a big deal. She doesn't like to waste her time. So I guess I should be clear. She's not indiscriminately kind. She'll size you up, and if she deems you worthy, she will talk to you.

She doesn't really give a shit about too many kids at school, but she does act weird around Ian. Instead of walking headlong through the crowd of kids gathering around the bulletin board between classes, she pulled over to one side to let him pass.

She didn't exactly do anything differently, but the air around her seemed to press in as she watched him go.

"Problem?" I asked.

"Yes," she said. But she didn't elaborate. She does things like that a lot.

She came over last night for dinner. It was my mom's idea. Actually, she just couldn't handle not meeting Maya for another second. No matter how many times I tell her we're just friends. She'd just smile in that annoying way she always does, like she knows something I don't. Then she'd wink.

I hate winking.

I made macaroni and cheese from scratch with broccoli and chicken. I didn't want to go too fancy, even though I make a wicked béarnaise sauce, because I didn't want to look like a douche. Anyway, Maya seemed to really like it.

"So, Maya, how did you and Adam meet?" Paul asked. My mom threw him a sharp look. I'd made her promise not to ask too many questions, and Paul had just wasted one that wouldn't give her any new information. Or so she thought.

"You saved her from drowning?" my mom shouted a few minutes later when Maya finished telling the story.

"Well, that actually wasn't the first time we met. I got lost on the first day, and she walked me to class," I said.

"Yeah," said Paul. "That's the more interesting story. You should lead with that."

Maya and my mom laughed, and I shrugged.

"You didn't tell me anything about this!" Mom protested, looking at me with indignation.

"Can't imagine why. I did kick him in the face while I was flailing around, so it's a good story," Maya said.

"Maybe he thought you'd ask too many questions, dear," Paul suggested lightly, sipping a glass of wine and raising his eyebrows at my mom. It wasn't nearly as awkward as I imagined it would be, and before long, Maya and I were shooed out of the kitchen so we could study for Academic Team.

I was responsible for straight memorization. Books, facts, dates, pop culture—the soft stuff. Maya would handle science and math—anything that needed to be figured out. Her eyes flicker over equations like they're works of art.

"Okay, you've seen the movie. Name the Vichy French police officer who helped Rick foil the Nazis' attempt to capture Laszlo and Ilsa at the end of *Casablanca*," she asked.

"That is not a question."

"It absolutely *is* a question."

"Well, it's really stupid. Why would anyone ever need to know that? How is it relevant to anything?"

"Do you know the answer or not?"

"Captain Louis Renault."

"Why would you criticize the question if you already know the answer?" she asked.

"Principle."

She rolled her eyes, but not the way other people do it. When Maya rolls her eyes, it looks like actual work. Like her eyeballs actually journey to the back of her skull before coming back to their sockets, and her hands sort of flutter like they're reaching for something less absurd. It means something when she does it. She's saying: *You are too stupid for words.*

"Name the play that the musical *My Fair Lady* is based on."

"*Pygmalion.* Do you think they'd actually ask that one?"

"Yes, it's one of the sample questions."

"Do you think they'd ask what insults Henry Higgins used to describe Eliza?"

"No. I don't."

Silence.

"What insults?" she asked.

"'Deliciously low'? 'Horribly dirty'? 'Squashed cabbage leaf'? 'Heartless guttersnipe'?" It was my grandma's favorite movie. I could recite it from start to finish.

"You're ridiculous," she said, scanning the quiz book. "Name the religion whose shrine often features barriers of rope called *shimenawa* to keep out demons."

She gave me a look that made me want to laugh. She meant it to be threatening, to remind me that we were studying for a reason, but it wasn't even remotely intimidating.

"Shinto." I said it with a straight face.

It was easy to annoy her when she was trying to be serious, but she never lost her temper. It went on like this for a while. She'd ask questions, I'd try to distract her, and then we'd end up talking about something else. The something else was my favorite part. She rolled her eyes a lot.

"Favorite movie?" I asked her.

"*When Harry Met Sally,*" she said without missing a beat.

"You can't be serious."

"I like the last scene," she said. "The line where he tells her he loves her."

"But it's not . . . I dunno. Not what I expected you'd like."

To be honest, I'd pictured Maya liking something a little bit less romantic. Something practical, solid. A documentary, maybe. Not something so cliché. It's one of my mom's favorites, which is why I'd seen it a few dozen times. Not seen it as in actually *watched* it, seen it as in absorbed it into my brain whenever it was on TV because my mom always liked to have a movie on for background noise.

"All women like that scene," she said without looking up from her flash cards. "If they say they don't, they're lying."

She says exactly what she means or she says nothing at all. But I still think it's odd that she can relate to Sally in the movie. Maya is serious and methodical. Not the sort of person who would fake an orgasm in a deli.

We text every day now. Nothing important. Sometimes it's just random facts I come across when I'm studying for Academic Team.

Me: Ben Franklin liked to take air baths for his health. He would sit in front of his window in the nude, presumably to get the full effects of the increased airflow.

A few seconds later, Maya texted back.

Maya: Ben Franklin was a sexy beast.

I really like her.

We got a new cross for the bell tower this week. Apparently the negotiations for the cross had been under way for months. Parishioners donated money to get it here from Italy. Even the local news station had agreed to do a piece on it when it arrived. Let it be known that religious people spend a lot of money on stupid shit.

Because this was an auspicious occasion (but mostly because the sisters wanted to watch, too), we were all allowed to gather outside the church as the cross was loaded onto the crane with care. Maya, Dwight, and I stood outside our history class in the center of the courtyard.

"Oh man, they're gonna drop it," Dwight kept saying under his breath. One of the nuns shushed him.

"Shut up. They're not going to drop it," I said.

"Man, it's going down," Dwight whispered.

Father Benjamin blessed it, of course, and was leading all of us in prayer when one of the cables snapped and the cross fell onto the roof with a deafening thud.

"I told you!" Dwight hissed. Maya stifled a laugh.

The news cameras kept rolling. No one spoke for several minutes. The man operating the crane looked like he was going to crap himself. It might have been the most exciting moment of our Catholic school education.

They eventually loaded it back onto the crane and got it locked in place, but as we walked back to class, I couldn't help but think that Jesus was trying to make a break for it.

DOSAGE: 1.5 mg. Same dosage. Less responsive than usual.

OCTOBER 17, 2012

You're persistent. I'll give you that. Other shrinks might wait patiently for a nonresponsive patient to open up, but you've changed your approach every session.

Games were a good idea. Darts, Jenga, chess, Nerf basketball . . .

Impressive.

And it does make for a less boring hour in your pretentious little office. One might argue that games could prompt me to open up and feel more comfortable around you. So I'll put your mind at ease.

I am comfortable with you. You haven't done anything wrong. There are even moments when you're not that annoying. But I'm still not going to talk to you. Just let me keep this tiny bit of control, okay?

You asked about our first official Academic Team practice.

The team is led by Sister Helen. She's an elderly woman with thick glasses who, in addition to devoting her life to the church, nurses a soft spot for Elvis Presley. She's also built like a linebacker. As far as nuns go, she's pretty laid-back, though. I've never heard her give a fire-and-brimstone speech. Which is basically the nuns' bread and butter. If they can't scare you with hell, there's nothing left. Maybe venereal disease.

We start every team meeting with a prayer, which shouldn't bother me, but it does because there's no reason to pray before we answer useless trivia questions. If God is real, he doesn't care. He's busy with other stuff that actually matters.

I could feel Maya's eyes on me during the prayer and realized that by now she probably has some sense of what I'm thinking by my expressions. *Aside from the fear that everyone will discover my secret.* We talk a lot. And besides my mom and now Dwight, she's probably the person I spend most of my time with. Well, *real* person.

So anyway, she looked at me like she knew I thought the prayer was stupid. And she gave me a look that clearly said *Shut up.* I almost wanted to say, *I didn't say anything!* But neither had she. I'd just had the whole conversation in my head. So I kept it to myself.

And actually, I'd really wanted to say, *But I would be proud to partake of your pecan pie,* in the stupid voice Billy Crystal uses in *When Harry Met Sally* because I wanted to make her laugh. You can YouTube it if you have no idea what I'm talking about. I love making her laugh. But actually, I'm glad I didn't say that out loud. It's pretty stupid. Rebecca nodded in agreement from the front of the room.

Practices are Tuesdays and Thursdays. After we pray, we split into two teams, and then Sister Helen asks the questions. We have buzzers that light up when the first person rings in and an electronic scoreboard that keeps track of points. As a group, we tally up all the points we get per category.

Speaking of the group, I'm pleased to say I am definitely not the most awkward member. The two girls Maya eats lunch with (who now also eat lunch with us), Clare and Rosa, sat down next to Maya on the other team. They both have noticeably bushy eyebrows and unmanageable hair pulled back into tight ponytails. Rosa is a question talker whose voice rises at the end of every sentence, while Clare talks so softly she's almost always asked to repeat her answers. And of course Dwight was there, too. It's unlikely that I will ever have another experience at this school without Dwight.

Five minutes into practice, it was clear that this had

nothing to do with Dwight wanting to be there because I was there. He'd been on the team for years. He basically knows everything. I probably could've buzzed in on a few questions, but Dwight was so fast it was impossible to match him. I just watched his finger bounce up and down on the buzzer for a while, before it started feeling too intimate and I had to look away. I should've asked if he and the buzzer wanted to be alone.

Sister Helen fired endless streams of questions that the rest of the pale kids raced to answer. Maya was the brains behind every chemistry and physics question for their side while Dwight methodically doodled math proofs on his scratch paper like a heroin addict getting his fix.

I won't lie. In those few instances when I can actually buzz in and answer something, it feels pretty good. The questions I answer are almost always the useless memorized trivia crap that I study with Maya, but still, I serve a purpose.

Dwight's mom and Maya's dad were both waiting for them when practice was over, so I had to wait a few minutes on my own before my mom got there to pick me up. I could've walked home, but it was dark out already.

It's weird being at school after hours. There's something eerie about the way the empty halls look sad when they're not filled with kids. I blinked that thought out of my mind pretty quickly because the last thing my mind needs is a terrifying image of a living, breathing school building.

I'm not afraid of the dark. There can't be any hallucinations if I can't see anything. But that's when the voices take over.

The drug helps. I don't believe them anymore. The voices just kind of flicker in my head, telling me to do things. If I believed them like I used to . . . they would be terrifying.

Usually it's a woman's voice, but that night after practice, it was a man's.

She deserves a normal kid, doesn't she, Adam? Someone who doesn't hear voices. Someone who doesn't make her new husband want to hide all the knives in the kitchen. What happens when your mother is dead and the drug stops working? What happens if Paul doesn't want you around anymore, and your mom has to choose between him or you? Do you think she's going to side with the kid who screams at nothing and closes all the blinds in the house like a vampire? You are a selfish, spoiled asshole, Adam. You don't deserve the love your mother gives you. You don't deserve the fancy new school your stepfather pays for. And someday soon, everyone at your new school is going to see there's something wrong with you. They're going to see what you're hiding. You won't be able to live a normal life anymore. You won't be able to run away.

You'll be doing everyone a favor if you just swallow the whole bottle of pills in your mom's locked cupboard and end it all. You know where she keeps the key. No one wants you around.

I closed my eyes and clenched my fists and did exactly what you tell me to do when I hear the voices. I took deep breaths and said the same thing over and over again. *Not Real Not Real Not Real Not Real Not Real Not Real Not Real Not Real.* Eventually, the voice went away and I saw the headlights of my mom's car as she rounded the corner into the parking lot.

It's the drug that makes the voices go away. Not the mantra. I know that. There's no reason to think that saying something over and over again is going to make a difference. It doesn't.

When we got home, Mom asked if I wanted to pull the car into the driveway.

I didn't want to.

I know that's weird and I get that I have enough weird things about me as it is without adding normal teenage weirdness to it, but I don't want to get my license. Dwight and Maya don't really care. They don't mind driving me around if I need a lift, and I have my permit because my mom insisted. But I don't drive if I can help it. And I actually don't get what the big deal is. It's not like I'm trapped if I don't drive. I can walk almost everywhere in this town without breaking a sweat. It's not exactly a sprawling metropolis.

I like being able to look out the window without worrying if I'm going to accidentally hit a hobo if I take my eyes off the road.

I don't actually think I'd hit a hobo, but I might hit a squirrel or someone's dog, and to be honest, I think I might feel worse about that. Running over a dog would suck because they're kind of like babies. Someone else is responsible for them, and I'd feel sad about killing something so helpless. Then I'd immediately be mad at the dumbass who let it get out of their yard.

Maya sent me a text that night.

Maya: Remember when you jumped into the pool and saved my life?

Me: Vaguely.

Maya: What went through your mind?

Me: That it would be nice if you didn't drown. What were you thinking?

Maya: How grateful I was that you showed up.

Me: Glad to be of service, ma'am. *hat tilt*

Maya: Was that all you were thinking?

I decided not to mention that at the time I wasn't one hundred percent sure she was real.

Me: No. I also thought you looked ridiculous clinging to the swimming lanes like a drowning cat. What 16-year-old doesn't know how to swim?!

Maya: You, sir, are an ass.

Me: Seriously though. How does someone who knows practically everything not know how to swim?

Maya: Easy. My parents tried to get me to take swimming lessons and I refused.

Me: How old were you?

Maya: Four.

Me: You were four and you just refused?

Maya: Yep.

Me: You really need to learn to swim.

Maya: I'll just avoid water.

Me: And when the ice caps melt?

Maya: Then you better be around to save me.

Me: Is that why you like me then? Because I saved your life that one time?

Maya's response was delayed and I realized I'd said something stupid. She'd never actually said she liked me. I'd just made it awkward.

But then she finally texted back.

Maya: Nope. It's cuz you're tall.

Sweet relief.

Me: Really? My heroism meant nothing?

Maya: Nope. Definitely the tall thing.

Me: But I'm also better-looking than Ian Stone, right?

Maya: *sighs* Yeah, I probably shouldn't tell you things.

Me: Nite, Maya.

Maya: Nite.

Sometimes I really do think I'm at my most charming in writing.

Do you agree, Doc?

DOSAGE: 1.5 mg. Same dosage. Subject's discussion of suicide in previous entry has been noted. No action necessary at this time.

OCTOBER 24, 2012

Paul drove me to school yesterday. I would've thought it was my mom's idea, but I heard him ask her if it was okay for him to take me. He made small talk on the way, and he's developed this weird habit of cracking his knuckles on the steering wheel by pressing all his fingers all the way back, which is really annoying.

"So, Academic Team practice with Maya later?"

"Yep."

Neither of us wanted to acknowledge that things were different. He'd dated my mom for a long time before they got married. And he never made me feel like a third wheel. He didn't treat me like a nuisance. In fact, for a long time it seemed like he actually kind of liked me.

When he found out I liked baking, he bought me a stand mixer. Which is awesome and not even remotely girlie. Don't judge me unless you have some idea of what a pain in the ass it is to mix cookie dough with a hand mixer.

Once we even had a moment watching *Indiana Jones and the Last Crusade* where we both did a Sean Connery impression at exactly the same time during the part when he says, "Goose-stepping morons like yourself should try reading books instead of burning them!" We both laughed.

There's a giant divide between us now. I went from being the stepson he actually sort of got along with to the monster they had to watch at all times. I know what he sees when he looks at me. I know what he must be thinking. It's why he cracks his knuckles. To keep himself from saying things he knows he shouldn't say.

Like what he told my mom when he found out. I can still remember what he said: "Maybe we should think about sending him to a place that can handle him."

When we got to school, he handed me money for lunch, which I stuffed in my pocket even though my meals were already prepaid. And I got out and walked down the grassy slope toward school.

Paul was still sitting in the car when I looked back. I waved and he waved back. Maybe this is just how it is now.

I can still hear him.

"Maybe we should think about sending him to a place that can handle him."

Sometimes I'm jealous of people with regular problems. At school I see the self-conscious girls worrying about their hair or if their legs look fat, and I just want to scream. Someone should tell them their problems are stupid.

I get that I'm not supposed to say that. Everyone you meet is fighting a harder battle, right? But what if they're not? What if the biggest thing they have to worry about is homework and whether they get into a good college? Even if they've lost a family member or their parents are getting a divorce or they're missing someone far away. That is not worse than having to take medication to be in control of your own mind. It's just not.

It's a very strange reality when you can't trust yourself. There's no foundation for anything. The faith I might have had in normal things like gravity or logic or love is gone because my mind might not be reading them correctly. You can't possibly know what it means to doubt everything. To walk into a room full of people and pretend that it's empty because you're not actually sure if it is or not.

To never feel completely alone even when you are.

I bet you can walk into a Starbucks and order a drink without wondering if the music playing on the speakers is playing for everyone or just in your head. But I guess

I should just be proud of myself because I don't avoid going places or doing things simply because I'm not sure if what's going on is real. If it's real, then I'm just living my life and responding to the world the only way I can. If none of this is real, then I'm still just living my life. And anyway, it's real to me.

St. Agatha's Church is open to the public during school hours, which means anyone can be there. The prayer room off to the right of the altar and the bathroom in the main hall are pretty much fair game for the homeless. The stalls in the bathroom are covered in graffiti that is cleaned up at the end of every month by kids serving detention.

The last time I used it, there were only two things written on the wall.

One was written in all caps in a delicate scrawl.

It read:

JESUS LOVES YOU.

The other, just below it, read:

Don't be a homo.

I can't really tell if that was in response to JESUS LOVES YOU. I think it must be. Weird notes to leave on a bathroom wall.

Weird notes to leave anywhere, really.

DOSAGE: 1.5 mg. Same dosage. Despite numerous attempts to engage Adam in conversation, he has remained silent during every session. Will continue to monitor body language for signs of receptivity to treatment. Will advise increase in dosage.

OCTOBER 31, 2012

It's Halloween, which basically means nothing if you go to St. Agatha's because no one in high school wears costumes. Maya told me that sometimes the little kids in the lower grades dress up, but they can only come as animals, plants, or their favorite saint. So, worst Halloween themes ever, I think.

She still remembers the one little girl who dressed up as a giant red rose one year and was so embarrassed when she got to school that she called her mom from the nurse's office to come pick her up because she was the only one in costume. I like the way she tells stories without adding any details that aren't strictly necessary. She gets to the point.

But I'm almost positive *she* was the little girl in that story and she didn't want to relive the embarrassment of the giant plastic flower headdress. Telling it like it happened to someone else might have made it less traumatizing for her. I get that. I like to pretend weird shit happens to other people, too. Unfortunately, that's not always possible.

I've started paying more attention to the side effects of other drugs. There's no question that we are overly medicated as a country. Our obsession with erections alone is just insane. You can barely watch cartoons anymore without bearing witness to some guy's embarrassing lack of wood.

And yes, I can almost hear your judgment: *But, Adam, without your current medication, wouldn't you be listening to the voices in your head and trying to follow the white rabbit to Wonderland?* Touché, jackass. Yes, you're right. Some people do need medication to help them get through some really serious shit, and I for one would not begrudge any man the opportunity to sport a raging boner whenever he feels like it.

When Paul and I were watching TV (actually, while I was watching TV and Paul was trying to think of something to say to me), I counted four commercials for sexual-enhancement drugs, one for depression, and one for restless legs syndrome. The side effects of all these drugs could be a number of things, like heart attack, anxiety, trouble urinating, an erection lasting longer than four hours, muscle tension, death, and, my favorite, anal leakage.

Death I understand. There are plenty of people willing to die to achieve ridiculous results. But I really don't think any drug could justify the possibility of anal leakage. If anything ever drips out of my ass as a result of the treatment I'm receiving, the cure is clearly not worth it. Please kill me.

I've been keeping a list of things that bother me. I'm not sure what prompted this except that I wanted it noted somewhere.

1. When people borrow my books and dog-ear pages.
2. The sound of a spoon scraping the bottom of a plastic yogurt cup.
3. Chewing with your mouth open. Gum. Food. Anything. This is completely unacceptable.
   *Note: Ian does this and it is disgusting.
4. Arguing with stupid people, knowing that you're right, but then they say something condescending that basically means, *Okay, I'm going to go because*

you don't seem to understand what I'm saying, when really you *do* understand—you just know that they're wrong. Like when someone says the world is flat and you argue with them because obviously it is not, so eventually they just smile and say something like, *Oh well, in some places that may be true.* You don't need to concede their point. There is no point. You should be allowed to slap them because clearly they are too stupid to live.

5. The word "rural." I will never use it. Ever. I hate the way it sounds.

6. When people ask me how I feel today.

DOSAGE: 2 mg. Increased dosage approved.

NOVEMBER 7, 2012

I don't even want to tell you about this, but I will because I have no one else to tell, and if I keep going over it in my own head, I'm going to go crazy.

Ha.

Maya was having a really bad day, but because she's basically a robot, she didn't want to tell me what was wrong. I don't mean robot as in she doesn't have any connection to people or that she doesn't care about anyone, because she does, she definitely does. I just mean that she processes information exactly as it hits her, as logically as possible. She doesn't make a fuss about it. She just responds to it. And she doesn't talk about her feelings. I don't think she would even use the word "feelings."

So I spent most of the day trying to figure her out,

which seemed to annoy her more than anything. And not in a cute way.

"Why won't you tell me what's wrong?" I asked her after class for what felt like the hundredth time that day.

"Just drop it, okay?" she hissed.

Her lips were pursed, and after our last class was over, she bolted to the library without looking back.

"What's wrong with her?" Dwight asked me.

"No idea. She wouldn't say."

"Is she . . . you know . . . ?" He looked mortified for asking the question.

"Dude. How would I know that?"

He shrugged, but I wondered inwardly if he had a point. Still, I'm pretty sure you aren't supposed to mention a girl's period. Ever.

It was one of those moments where you just know you should be doing something, but you're not sure what. Maya was clearly upset, but since she wouldn't tell me what was wrong, my options were limited. I sat at my desk for a minute waiting for the class to clear out when I had a thought.

Rebecca was twirling like she always does when I think I have a good idea. She did cartwheels on the lawn in front of me.

Spontaneity. Girls like that, right?

I stopped at the grocery store and went straight to

Maya's house, knowing she wouldn't be home for a couple hours. She was doing research at the library. I'd seen her through the window. She'd said her computer at home was too slow and usually monopolized by her little brothers.

I'd been there a couple times to drop her off with my mom after Academic Team, but I'd never gone inside. The neighborhood was older, and some of the houses were pretty beat up. Dead grass, plastic flamingos. Short chain-link fences around the front yard. That kind of thing.

Her dad answered when I knocked, and one of her brothers drove a plastic trike into a wall somewhere behind him. Maya had said her dad was a plumber. When I saw his face, I knew that Maya must take after her mom. There was nothing in the goofy face and untucked shirt that could have belonged to Maya.

I'd never officially met the guy before, and I hadn't considered that what I wanted to do would be weird coming from a stranger. He was maybe five foot six, so I sort of towered over him with my bag of groceries, but when I explained what I wanted to do, his face split into a wide grin. Maya had told him about me. Most people would have looked at me funny, but there was something in his expression that made me feel like he honestly didn't think I was doing anything weird. That made me feel good for some reason. So I walked into their small kitchen and got to work, while Rebecca sat at one of the barstools with a dreamy expression on her face.

Two hours later, Maya walked through the front door with a defeated-sounding "I'm home." Her dad and brothers were already sitting down at the table, which was overflowing with some of my best work.

Her hair had mostly fallen out of her ponytail, and her uniform looked like old skin she wanted to shed. I could tell she'd been crying. Then she asked what was going on.

One of her brothers answered in a high-pitched shriek. "Adam made dinner!" They're both roughly the same size and look like the same person, so I haven't gotten their names right yet. I mean, I know they're called David and Lucas, but I have not yet tried to assign the correct name to the correct kid.

I walked over to her, took her backpack off her shoulders, and pulled out a chair at the table. She sat down and didn't say a word while her dad filled her in on how long I'd been in the kitchen, that I'd wanted to surprise her . . . etc., etc. He was excited as he told the story, but she just nodded like a zombie while her brothers took turns making a mess on the tablecloth. Some of the food got into their mouths, I think.

It was my go-to meal. The one I make because it's simple and impressive. Classic lasagna, garlic knots with oil and vinegar, tomato and mozzarella salad, and fried zucchini. Then brownies with ice cream for dessert because I didn't have time for tiramisu. Which is a shame because my tiramisu is a religious experience. Seriously.

Her dad had a giant grin on his face during the whole meal, but Maya, I couldn't read. I made a plate for Maya's mom and covered it in tinfoil before saying good night to everyone. Maya's dad shook my hand, gave me a bear hug, and told me to come back anytime. Her brothers both hugged me around the knees before shouting something incomprehensible and racing down the hall to avoid a bath that, by the smell of them, they clearly needed.

Maya still hadn't said anything. I figured my plan had been a complete disaster. I told her I'd see her at school and started walking home. Just as I was about to turn the corner, she came running up behind me.

"Why did you do that?" she asked.

"Do what? Make dinner?"

"Yes. Why did you make dinner?"

I shrugged. "Because all I can do is listen and feed you. And you weren't talking. So I made dinner."

"But . . . why?" Her voice sort of cracked.

"Because you said it was mostly scrambled eggs or whatever you felt like making when you got home. I thought it would be nice."

"You thought it would be nice or you felt sorry for me?" I flinched at the forced toughness in her voice.

"What? No! I don't feel sorry for you!" What the hell was wrong with her?

"Really? Is that why you came to our house in our ghetto neighborhood to bring food to poor people?" I'd never seen Maya like this before. Her hair had completely fallen out of its ponytail, and her eyes were searching my face for an explanation I couldn't give. I had no idea what to say.

"That isn't why I came," I whispered.

"Then why would you come to our house and make dinner?" she asked again.

"Because I thought it would make you happy, and I like making you happy!" I shouted. I think we were both a little surprised by how loud my voice was. I don't shout if I can help it, and I actually can't remember the last time I raised my voice to make a point. I'm tall and I've always understood that the height coupled with yelling is fairly intimidating to regular-sized people. She stared at me for a few seconds.

That was when she kissed me full on the mouth, which turned out to be quite a feat because of the height difference. She pulled my face to hers and kissed me like she was trying to breathe and I was hogging all the air. I wrapped my arms around her and lifted her up onto her toes. A full minute might have passed like this before she pulled away and said, "It *did* make me happy."

She didn't look serious. In fact, in that moment she looked more un-Maya-ish than I'd ever seen her.

Then she turned and ran back toward her house so I wouldn't notice that she was crying.

When I walked home, I heard a train whistle, and even though I knew no trains were running and it wasn't real, I smiled. I like trains.

Remember when I said that in stories trains mean either adventure or death? Maybe it's more than that. They might also mean choice. Every time the train's whistle blows, it's like a call to do something. I just don't know what.

My mom was worried and angry when I got home, because I'd forgotten to tell her where I was going or that I was going to be late. Well, she's probably always secretly hoped for regular kid problems.

Came in after curfew. Check.

I texted Maya while I was getting ready for bed.

Me: Are you ever going to tell me what you were upset about today?

A few minutes passed before she responded.

Maya: Ian

Me: What about him?

Maya: His family pays for my scholarship at St. Agatha's

Me: Ok . . .

Maya: They do a yearly audit of my school records to make sure my grades are good. But today Ian was there at the meeting for the first time ever. It's usually just the family's financial planner who checks all the requirements off a list, but Ian pulled my records out himself. And went through everything out loud. Personal stuff. Mom's salary. Dad's salary. Financial hardship eligibility. I was so mad I was crying.

Me: Is there anything I can do?

I wanted to hurt him.

Maya: I'll just trust karma. Besides, I'm not so angry about it right now.

See? Food fixes everything.

Well, *good* food, anyway.

DOSAGE: 2 mg. Same dosage.

NOVEMBER 14, 2012

I've told my mom that I don't need therapy, but she doesn't believe me. All my doctors still recommend it. They insist that this is the only outlet I have for the side effects of the drug.

The other doctors like to test my memory. But as I've told you, my memory is excellent. I can recite most major speeches if I like the way they sound.

It's the other shit that's messy.

Luckily, we seem to have hit the sweet spot for this drug because I can almost will my delusions to leave.

Yesterday, while I was talking to Maya, I watched the mobsters step out of the shadows on the blacktop and raise their guns. Just as they were about to open fire, I felt something strange snap into place in my head. It was the greatest sense of control I've ever had.

I was able to stare down the mob boss until he didn't seem real anymore. He blinked. The mobsters and their weapons sank into the asphalt and disappeared.

I did that. I made them leave for the first time in my life.

Anyway, you asked about my Academic Team meets. They usually take place on the stage in the auditorium. Dwight says Ian's family shelled out a ton of money about ten years ago to rebuild it. Now other Catholic high schools travel to us because our facilities are better. In fact, it's so fancy that politicians want to use it for debates.

It's weird to describe an event where you know that everyone else is smarter than you. There are really only three options: get intimidated, get competitive, or watch.

For most of the match, I watched from the second-string bench while Maya dominated the science questions and Dwight answered everything else. I don't notice this much during school anymore—maybe it was the lighting on the stage or something—but he's really pale. So pale you can almost see his brain through his forehead.

In the audience, I saw his mom, who looked a little older than the other parents. I'd heard her talk to Dwight before our practices. She's definitely the overprotective type. You can just tell by the way she watches him compete onstage. I looked back to the stage when she started to wave at the team, and Dwight waved awkwardly back, clearly embarrassed. Maya was sitting next to him, and she smiled at me.

It was a very different smile now. I tried not to feel too cocky about that, but it was a sort of powerful feeling knowing that I could make her smile. Every time it lit up her face, she looked more beautiful than ever. The next thought that consumed me was that she was mine. We kissed. We had the boyfriend/girlfriend label conversation. Everything is now legit.

Maya never actually demanded a label. She never insisted on having "the talk" about our relationship, but we ended up having it anyway because of Dwight. We were eating lunch, and out of nowhere he asked the question. "So are you guys like a couple now?" And before I could swallow my food and think of something clever to say in response to this, Maya said yes, without giggling like an idiot or adding anything else to the conversation. Dwight smiled at us, then went back to eating his organic, vegan lunch, with the school paper propped up against his water bottle.

"We are?" I asked.

"Unless you don't want to be," she said.

"No! I do," I said a little too enthusiastically.

"Good," she said.

"Yeah, good."

And that was how the pathetic conversation happened. Clare and Rosa both giggled but didn't say anything. Our new status had been declared like a proclamation. The kind that signals high school intimacy in a way that nothing else can.

I should probably add here that Maya and I haven't done anything yet, and I'm telling you because it feels like the kind of thing that might make me seem like a regular guy. Because it isn't that I don't *want* to do anything, but she isn't ready. And that's fine because I'm not the kind of guy who pushes to do things with a girl. The kind of things we all think about in the shower.

But yes, I think about sex. A lot. It's just more than that. There's this feeling that I have to be near her because she makes me less afraid, less angry, less paranoid that someone is going to find out about me and sound the alarm to remove the crazy guy.

In a lot of ways, she's the thing that keeps me sane. More than the drug or the therapy. She's the cure. That was all I could think about while I doodled on my scratch paper and listened as my team answered questions.

Then something weird happened. Dwight got a massive nosebleed and had to be escorted off the stage. I guess it wasn't actually weird because he's gotten them at practice before, but this time it spurted out of his nostrils like a geyser. Torrents of blood gushed down his face and onto his ridiculous short-sleeved collared shirt that made him look like a traveling Mormon. As if she had been waiting for something like this to happen, his mother raced up the stairs and onto the stage, pulled a heavy-duty plastic container of Kleenex out of her bag, and stuffed a tissue into his nostrils. Poor Dwight.

Once he was carted off, Sister Helen grabbed me by the collar and practically threw me into Dwight's empty chair so the competition could continue.

Maya smiled her usual serious smile (because she was onstage), and then she squeezed my thigh. Her hand lingered there for a moment, then moved back onto the table.

I don't remember breathing after that. I'm sure I did—I just don't remember doing it. For the next few moments, I wasn't really onstage with the rest of my team. I was in my head, somewhere alone with Maya.

"Adam, pay attention!" Sister Helen hissed at me.

No one had seen Maya touch me. She barely hid her smile behind her hair as she bent forward to work out a problem. No one suspects her of anything devious. Probably because she looks innocent. It's incredibly misleading.

Then a strange haze fell over me. I knew something was off because after the moderator called for silence, I could still hear voices. They were soft at first, and then they got louder.

They were giving me answers.

Capital of Burkina Faso?

"Ouagadougou," they said.

What character in Shakespeare's *Othello* . . .

"Iago!" they shouted.

I was on a roll. I was buzzing in faster than anyone else. Dwight watched from the audience with a dazed expression on his face while his mom tried to soak up the blood. Maya's eyes were wide with shock. My mom and Paul were wearing similar expressions of fear mixed with what appeared to be pride. And I knew why. Every question I answered was golden, but I'd never been this quick on the buzzer at practice. I must have looked manic.

The voices got louder until, quite suddenly, the buzzer signaling the end of the match sounded. We'd won by over sixty points.

But the voices didn't stop. They kept growing louder until I couldn't hear my own voice and couldn't concentrate over the sound of my pale, nerdy, cheering teammates, who were all as shocked as I was that their lowest scorer at practice had just miraculously out-geeked them all. I knew how to pretend. I just nodded and smiled at everyone, even though I couldn't hear a word they were saying.

Sister Helen looked pleased as well. She was eating a cookie as she chatted up Father Benjamin. Maya was obviously surprised, but she had a big grin on her face.

Then I saw my mom and watched her face fall. Her eyes said it all.

Be careful. Are you okay?

The voices stopped and I could think again.

Maya and I went out for coffee afterward. I guess I would consider it our first official date.

Actually, she had coffee. I had juice. I bake with coffee, but I don't drink it. I hate stuff that smells better than it tastes. Seems ass-backward.

Maya likes it, though. She says when she drinks it on the weekends, it's the only time her brothers leave her alone. For some reason, the "don't bother me until I'm done with my coffee" seems to work on them.

Anyway, there was a moment of awkwardness. We sat down at a table at Starbucks, and I kissed her. Well, tried to.

"Did you just kiss my eye?" she asked, squinting up at me. I'd leaned in a little too early, and as a result, I'd kissed her eyeball.

"Yeah," I said, laughing nervously. "Girls aren't into that?"

"No, that's totally hot," she said in a mock serious

tone, rubbing her eye. "But I prefer this." She put her hand on the back of my neck and pulled me toward her, kissing me hard on the mouth. When I started to pull away, she bit my lower lip and then gently let go.

"I prefer that, too," I said, still smiling. The biting thing was amazing, but I was a little freaked out by how advanced that move was. I thought it might be a good idea for me to say something really clever or romantic.

I tried to think of a cool way to tell her that coffee tasted better on her lips, but Maya pulled me in again before I could speak.

My mom and Paul are disgustingly cute sometimes.

They have a date night once a week. It was something my mom insisted on doing when Paul was made partner at his firm. She said she was feeling a little neglected when he started bringing more work home, and I think after my dad, Mom still has a hard time believing that Paul isn't going anywhere. But I don't.

It's the way he looks at her. My dad never looked at her like that. At least that I can remember. With the eyes and the grin. She doesn't have anything to worry about. Paul loves her.

Every once in a while, he'll surprise her and take her somewhere really special. He's even gone so far as to buy her a new outfit, lay it out for her, and tell her exactly what time to be ready for their date. Apparently, he's asked stores to save her size and brand preferences so he can continue to do this in the future. Barf, but yeah, okay. I get it. It's cute. Like that scene in *Field of Dreams* where we find out that Moonlight Graham bought all those blue hats for his wife, so many that when he died, they found boxes of them he never got a chance to give her.

He's also got the flowers thing down.

My mom once told him that she hated flowers. She couldn't understand why anyone would kill something so beautiful and give it as a gift only to watch it die slowly over the next few days. So Paul got creative. He bought paintings of flowers, had origami flowers made, bought her earrings in the shape of flowers. Once he even bought her cooking flour (which I used), and it made my mom laugh.

Mom does little things for him, too. She'll leave notes in the pockets of his clothes and slip chocolate into his lunch.

They're disgusting to the point that it is probably uncomfortable for people to be in their presence. But it can't be denied that they have something beautiful. It must be nice having someone to come home to every day. Someone to be gross with.

My mom is the kind of person who makes you feel important. No matter how tiny your problem is, she listens like it's a major crisis, and she wants to make everything okay. So she's great, but she is also the kind of person who stores soy sauce packets in the utensil drawer and forgets whether she left the garage door open. *Every day.* And Paul is the kind of guy who doesn't mind secretly throwing the soy sauce packets out and calling our elderly neighbor across the street to check that the garage door is closed. I'm glad he's patient.

I'm glad they have each other, but sometimes I think about how much happier everyone would be if I weren't around. That's when I feel sad and guilty because if anything happened to me, my mom would be devastated, but as long as I'm in her life, she's always going to worry about whether or not I'm okay. I don't know which is worse.

There are days I just wish I weren't me.

But if I weren't me, Maya would be texting someone else every night before she goes to bed.

Yesterday it was this:

Maya: Hey. Just thought I should tell you that I really like kissing you.

Me: I like that you like kissing me too.

Maya: Barf.

DOSAGE: 2 mg. Same dosage.

NOVEMBER 21, 2012

It was somehow decided that Dwight and I would play tennis on Monday nights. I do not play tennis. Nor have I ever expressed any desire to do so.

This is what happened.

During last week's Academic Team match, it only took a few minutes for my mom to make eye contact with Dwight's mom to see if Dwight was okay after his nosebleed. She walked over with Paul in tow and proceeded to rummage through her bag for wet wipes to help mop the blood off Dwight's face.

My mom still keeps wet wipes in her purse. They usually dry out before she has the opportunity to use them, but on the rare occasion that she can bust one out and wipe something sticky off her hands, she'll turn to me and raise an eyebrow as if to say, *See? I told you they'd come in handy.*

Whatever transpired between the two moms in that moment, I will never know. By the time I got in the car, it had been decided that I would spend more time with Dwight. I tried explaining that that was basically impossible, since he was already in almost all my classes AND on Academic Team, but my mom liked the idea of me hanging out with friends outside school. There was no dissuading her.

Being set up on a "playdate" in high school is not beyond the realm of behavior for my mother, but I still pretended to be shocked and outraged. Even though Paul tried to intervene, my mom was resolute. I would play tennis with Dwight.

So on Monday Dwight and I met at a tennis court near my neighborhood. The first thing I noticed was that he looked skinnier in tennis clothes than he did in his uniform at school.

"Have you ever played before?" he asked.

"Nope."

"Have you ever seen a tennis match before?"

"Nope."

He was unfazed. Dwight taught me how to hold a racket, and for one hour we hit balls back and forth to each other. He was actually really good, way more coordinated than I thought he'd be, which is probably pretty jerky on my part. When we were done, we sat on the edge of the tennis court for a while, drinking Gatorade. I noticed he was really quiet. It was weird.

"What's up?" I asked.

"Did you just come here because your mom told you to?" he asked. The question was awkward. I'd put it in the same category as *Will you be my friend?*

"No," I lied. "I've never played tennis before. It sounded like fun." His face split into this big, goofy grin.

"Same time next week?"

"Sure."

He picked up his bag and walked off the court, leaving a heavy scent of his sunscreen in the air. SPF 500, I'm sure.

And that was it. I don't know if we're just both so completely pathetic that our moms felt the need to set us up, or if Dwight and I were always meant to venture on this awkward journey of friendship together. But it's okay. I guess.

It is not generally my prerogative to bum anyone out. I don't want them to feel like they have to carry my problems around as if they don't already have shit of their own festering inside them. It isn't fair. That's why I always say "Fine" when my mom asks how I am and why I always return Paul's awkward smile with an equally awkward smile of my own. I do not want to be someone's problem. I don't want to be the reason someone has to change their life.

Today at school I thought about you. Not in a creepy way. I just wondered about the other people you've treated. The other schizos with their disjointed speech and soapy spit bubbles and tinfoil hats. The ones who aren't on ToZaPrex and who no longer see the line between what is real and what is batshit crazy.

About a year ago, when my mom first took me to see a doctor, I was in bad shape. It felt like my brain had been dumped onto a dirty sidewalk, then poured back into my head with bits of garbage and broken glass. It was surprising how quickly it happened. I was fine, and then I wasn't. The doctor's waiting room was like purgatory: everybody knows they're already dead, but it's such a depressing afterlife it's actually a little scary if you think about it too hard. Exactly like being stuck in line at the DMV for all eternity.

The waiting room is a place I still have nightmares about. Except when I do, I'm chained to one of the chairs and trying to ward off the punches of another patient while my mom watches from behind a glass window because a man in a white coat is trying to explain that I'm too dangerous to approach. I'm screaming and crying, but no one hears me or, worse, no one cares. It's the loneliest I've ever felt.

Anyway, the waiting room only had two or three patients in it. All men. Unless you counted Rebecca, who was sitting quietly and playing at the Lego table. One of the men was my age and with his mom. He looked like he was in worse shape than me, which was comforting for some reason. Of course, that made me feel guilty. Why should the fact that he looked worse off make me feel better about myself? It doesn't matter. There's no escape for either of us. Even our moms know this is true, which is probably the worst thing about this situation.

I'd rather suffer alone.

So the other kid in the waiting room was rocking back and forth and humming to himself. It wasn't a song I recognized, and the tune seemed to change sporadically. His mom wasn't saying anything to him about it. She was reading something on her Kindle and acting like her son was just sitting there not doing anything odd. It was like she knew her kid was being weird, but she would be more than happy to kick your ass if you brought it up. She had this Xena: Warrior Princess attitude about her that made it perfectly clear that she had been fighting for her son his entire life. It was only when he started pulling at his sleeve that she snapped to attention and pulled the sleeve back, but not before I saw the deep red gashes in his forearms. They looked like he'd been digging for something up to the crook of his elbow.

I was staring, and his mother noticed and glared back, daring me to say something, which kicked *my* mom's natural protective instincts into gear. They stared each other down for a moment before my mom asked, "Here to see Dr. Finkleman, too?"

The other woman nodded, touched her son's head fondly, and eventually resumed her reading. They were no longer adversaries, just two women fighting the same battle, putting their faith in the same doctor. *Cure my son.*

I think about that waiting room more than any other spot because it's our gathering place. The place where the crazies go. A group of us, seeing things no one else can see and following orders no one else can hear, because we have no choice. Our truth is different from everyone else's.

I guess I should count my blessings because I could have been born in pretty much any other decade in history and been sent to a madhouse where the patients were caged and baited like animals. Places so breath-takingly evil that you don't have to imagine hell. Asylums were nasty places.

This entry is a bummer, but count *your* blessings. At least you get paid to read it.

DOSAGE: 2.5 mg. Approved increase in dosage.

NOVEMBER 28, 2012

I used to think that Dwight's ability to talk in almost every circumstance was annoying, but I've developed a respect for it. It is almost impossible to keep up a steady stream of conversation during a tennis match, but Dwight does it without getting winded or breaking a sweat.

He would be perfectly content talking forever without ever actually saying anything. But the nice thing about him is he doesn't worry about how he looks to other people. He's awkward. Pale. Skinny. He's not the type to feel sorry for himself. And the weird thing is he's happy all the time, which is why it was so odd to hear the unhappiness in his voice after gym yesterday.

We'd just finished our laps on the track, and most of the guys had already showered. St. Agatha's does not have a long wall of showers like some of those locker rooms you might see on TV. They have individual stalls with hooks on the outside of the door for your clothes. Very classy . . . and phenomenally stupid for high school showers.

I'd been one of the last ones to finish the run, so when I walked into the locker room, all I could hear was Dwight pleading with Ian and four other guys to give him back his clothes.

"C'mon, guys," Dwight said through the door. Ian was wearing his towel around his waist and holding Dwight's clothes away from his body like a matador coaxing a bull into the arena.

"Seriously, guys. I'm going to be late for class," Dwight pleaded.

"Not really my problem," said Ian. He walked to the row of lockers right by the door to the main hallway and tossed Dwight's clothes high out of reach. "Looks like you don't have any options."

Being tall and menacing has its advantages. I don't think anyone saw me enter the room, so when I parted the crowd around Ian, there was silence. He was about to open his mouth to speak when I yanked off his towel and shoved him out the locker room door and into the hallway, holding the door tight so he couldn't get back in. He pounded on it from the other side, and, curiously, none of the other guys in the locker room did anything to stop me. In fact, they scattered when I looked back at them.

Then the bell rang.

The sound of hundreds of footsteps echoed in the hallway, followed by laughter. I grabbed Dwight's clothes from the top of the locker and handed them to him over his stall.

"You just pushed him into the hall stark naked," he said.

"Yep," I said. Dwight's face split into a grin.

"How did he look?"

"Cold," I said. "C'mon. We're going to be late."

It was probably immature and incredibly stupid, but some of the best moments are. I'd probably pay for it later. Still, no regrets.

Maya's text later:

Maya: I saw Ian Stone's white pimply ass today running past the gym. I almost went blind. I'm told you had something to do with that?

Me: You're welcome. Love, Karma.

DOSAGE: 2.5 mg. Same dosage.

DECEMBER 5, 2012

My mom is pregnant.

DOSAGE: 3 mg. Approved increase in dosage.

JANUARY 9, 2013

Let's just blow past the last thing I wrote for a minute. And while we're at it, I see no reason to devote any time to my family vacation (we went to Hawaii) or my Christmas gifts (they got me the deep fryer I wanted). I got Maya a life vest and swimming lessons. She handwrote all of her grandmother's Filipino recipes and gave them to me in a leather-bound book. Yes, of course I missed her while I was gone.

But none of that matters, because while I was gone, twenty kids and six adults were murdered at Sandy Hook Elementary School in Connecticut.

Around the world, this happens fairly regularly. People drop like flies by the thousands, and usually no one cares. No one here cares, anyway. Before you make that face, take a minute to acknowledge that I am right.

Because, honestly, who cares about a bunch of dead people you don't know? Nobody. Unless they're kids. Then we care, because that sucks.

Mom and Paul didn't tell me about the secret meeting they'd had with the school after it happened. I wouldn't have even known about it if I hadn't been looking at my mom's phone.

In this case, the school knew someone they could be afraid of. They knew someone they could blame if the danger were present. The head of the school board (Ian's dad) planned the meeting quickly after the shooting, because he needed to make sure no one else had to be notified, for legal reasons. And it was hard to do with Christmas only a few days away. Other parents wouldn't want their kids going to school with someone like me. Someone with the potential to lose control. Most people wouldn't even bother to research my condition or ask about my medication. They'd go straight to panic. I can't say I blame them.

Even though it happened on the other side of the country, I immediately knew what it would mean for me.

He was one of us.

And an honors student. He even went to Catholic school for a little while.

Eerily enough, we even have the same first name. Adam.

Even if all those things weren't true, there was no

way the school would not want to talk with my mom and Paul. I knew they'd want to have a board meeting, perhaps a public inquisition to keep things Catholic.

They objected to the secrecy. They wanted someone to protest the fact that Paul had made it abundantly clear that no one at school was to know about my condition. Because then if an "incident" occurred, there would undoubtedly be the parent who screamed bloody murder because they had not been told that their child was attending school with a ticking time bomb.

Me.

This conflicts with the church's actual teachings, though, which is highly inconvenient for them. The Bible teaches tolerance. I doubt that Jesus would have encouraged people to "out" me as a schizo. Does *Let him who is without sin be the first to cast a stone* ring any bells for anyone?

They don't know much about the shooter yet. He could have planned the whole thing for months, gotten other people involved, notified the police ahead of time to bargain for something he wanted. But none of that seemed to be the case. They're just speculating on the why. Which to me doesn't actually mean shit.

The facts are that a twenty-year-old man shot his mother and then walked into an elementary school and opened fire on children and teachers. Just destroyed them for no reason, as if they were in the way of something.

The discussion about guns is happening again, but nobody seems too concerned about changing any laws.

Nothing changes the fact that those kids are dead, forever.

My mom is a pretty sensible person and might've been crying a little bit about the gruesome deaths, but mostly she was crying about me. She watched the coverage on the news, and I just knew. Because this guy had mental problems and who knows what kind of demons whispering in his ear. She was afraid for me.

There might be a witch hunt of every person with a mental illness. It would be easy to make the homeless schizophrenic community disappear. No one would notice they were gone. And then the people who talk to themselves. The poor bastards who are bipolar. Everyone with severe behavioral problems. That is Mom's nightmare. That someday someone will come for me and she won't be able to stop them.

When I got back to school after Christmas break, we all talked about it. The first mass was dedicated to the victims and their families. A little, terrified-looking second grader who could barely see over the lectern read the Prayers of the Faithful. She spoke in a tiny voice and said, "For the victims of the Sandy Hook shooting and their families. Lord, hear our prayer."

When she was done speaking, there was this terrible emptiness. She was probably the same age as the kids who'd died, and I felt this overwhelming sadness that must have shown on my face, because Maya touched my hand.

Of course we had to talk about it when we got back to class. We'd have to openly discuss every detail of the event so we'd know what to do if anything like that happened here. There's no way the nuns would let us escape a long, drawn-out safety discussion accompanied by a prayer for the victims, because why not? We pray for every other stupid thing. I can't imagine why praying for the dead would be any less ridiculous. It was maybe half a second after the prayer that the class started talking about the shooter.

"What was wrong with him?" someone asked.

"They're not sure. Mental problems, they think." Sister Catherine's eyes did the tiniest of double takes in my direction as she said it, but she turned away quickly. Rebecca was sitting on Sister Catherine's desk at the front of the room, looking furious. If she'd been real, she would've thrown something at her. Then again, if she'd been real, I wouldn't be crazy.

That was when I heard it.

"Why didn't the fucker just kill himself if he was so miserable?"

I didn't see who'd said it, but I heard it. It was in a stage whisper, but Sister Catherine's head snapped up as she hissed "Who said that?" in a deadly voice. Her mouth stretched into a thin line as she glared out at the class.

No one moved. No one said a word. The phrase just hung in the air above us.

Why didn't the fucker just kill himself?

And for a second, I was angry because whoever had said it has no idea what it's like to lose control. They don't know what it's like to be haunted by your own mind. They don't understand the mad desire to make the voices stop even if it means doing what they tell you to. But I had to stop myself because I realized my reaction was in sympathy of the killer, and I didn't want it to be.

When the bell rang, Sister Catherine caught my attention and waved me over to her desk as quietly as possible. She waited until the class had cleared out before she spoke.

"They didn't mean you, Adam," she said quickly. Most of the time I can forget that the teachers know my secret, so it was odd having this discussion.

"They did," I said. "They just don't know they meant me."

She shook her head. "There is no justification for

anyone to take their own life. That power belongs to God alone."

"Then maybe he should have taken that guy out before he killed those kids," I said. Sister Catherine looked like she was looking for the right words, but I didn't want her to feel like she needed to comfort me. "It's okay, Sister. I'll see you tomorrow."

In this situation, whoever had said that in class was right. He could've just offed himself. No one else would've had to die.

I don't think I'll ever forget that feeling, when I learned what someone would say if they knew my secret. What they really thought about people with my condition. Not the fake comforting words they'd give that other people would hear. The real words in their heart.

If they knew I was a threat, they'd tell me to kill myself. They'd think I was a monster.

On Monday I'd received a friendly reminder notice from the office to check in with my student ambassador. Naturally, I tossed it in the trash. Nobody was actually monitoring my participation in the student ambassador program, but I was supposed to be having weekly meetings with Ian. I guess the prospect of these meetings disappeared when I shoved his naked ass into a crowded hallway. It's a shame because I think we were really starting to hit it off.

The weird thing was he'd been unusually quiet since then. I didn't worry about it until today, when I passed him in the hall after class. Instead of walking past me like I didn't exist, he stopped and looked at me with a weird expression on his face, like he knew something I didn't.

When I walked to the bathroom in the hallway next to the church, he followed me in and took the urinal next to me and started to take a leak. I usually avoid conversation with other guys while I have my dick in my hand, but Ian was unfazed. It was the first time I'd been this close to him since the shower incident.

"Tragic what happened in Connecticut," he said.

"Yeah," I said, watching his lip curl and waiting for him to get to the point.

"People with problems like that. We should just round them up and shoot 'em, you know? That way nobody gets hurt." He zipped up his pants and clapped me on the back, but not before turning to the JESUS LOVES YOU/ DON'T BE A HOMO graffiti on the wall and saying, "That's been there forever. Someone should really clean it up."

I felt my body go cold.

*   *   *

Sometimes I forget you're there. I write these notes and spill my guts and sometimes it feels like you really hear me. Other times it feels like I'm just writing to nobody.

So I'd like to take this opportunity to say that I don't like guns. I don't own guns and I don't have any desire to shoot anyone ever. I don't play violent video games, mostly because I'm bad at them. I don't even really like laser tag.

Amen.

DOSAGE: 3 mg. Same dosage.

JANUARY 16, 2013

Yes, I understand that you want to know how I hurt my hand. And I get that this isn't how therapy works. I'm not getting the full benefits of the session by talking to you through these "diary" entries, because therapy is a conversation, not a dissertation. You listen to me, we talk about what I've said, and then we make a plan to do it all over again the following week, and nobody ever gets fixed.

The thing is that I know what's going on. I don't need you to tell me what's wrong with me. I don't need the back-and-forth analysis of what my dreams are telling me or how my hallucinations are changing. I'm very aware of the things lurking in my head. I understand that I'm not normal, so I actually don't need you, which is why I don't need to talk in your office.

I don't ask you about the picture frames on your desk of your three children, who will all most definitely need braces. (Sorry, dude, but it's true.) I don't ask you about your wife or about the painting behind your desk of the woman with the green umbrella.

It might actually be worse for you because I write everything down. It means the evidence is all here. If you miss my descent into madness, overlook some anecdote that seems off, it could be crucial. It could be the difference between failure and success. You're supposed to notice this stuff before it happens.

So you also asked me about my mom. What I think about the pregnancy, if I'm worried. I guess that's fair. Major life changes are supposed to set us off. Any disruption in our day-to-day routine could cause problems, which is why my mom has been watching me more closely than ever.

My mom had me pretty young. Twenty is young to be a mom. That's four years from now for me. I can't imagine having a kid in four years.

But I guess it makes sense that she and Paul want to have a baby. The funny thing is they didn't talk to me about it. My mom usually goes into excruciating detail about everything, so it's really out of character for her to keep this kind of secret. They waited until she was three months in to tell me.

When they told me about it, Paul looked anxious, like he was afraid the news would set me off, which made Rebecca cry, because why would a baby set me off?

It's sad that my mom's worry is split between her thoughts about the baby and her thoughts about me. She shouldn't be worrying about me at all. Plus I can hear Paul's reaction in my head. Metaphorically, of course—I don't actually hallucinate his voice. He's got his own kid to protect now. It's an almost Shakespearean turn of events, where I should be cast out because I pose a threat to the true heir.

It's nice that I can talk to Maya about the pregnancy, at least. Her brothers are only five, so she understands what it's like to be a lot older than your siblings.

I think it's weird that I still haven't seen Maya's mom. She's a nurse and works strange hours, but still I feel like I should have bumped into her by now.

Okay. So my hand. This is what happened.

Maya and I decided to stay late at the library after school on Thursday to work on some homework because Paul had to work late and my mom had a doctor's appointment. It was kind of a date. I brought gummy bears and she had peanut butter pretzels. If food is required for it to be classified as a date, then there you have it.

I like libraries, if for no other reason than they give homeless people a place to hang out. There's something nice about the way you're never too old to go into one, but it still makes you feel the way it did when you were small. I still remember how my mom would let me wander the children's book section while she looked in the career section for jobs for my dad.

And I like the smell of books.

A few minutes after I arrived, I noticed Ian staring at me. He had his feet up on a nearby table, and his eyebrows were raised. I'd unknowingly started twiddling the pen in my right hand to ward off the group of flies that were circling my stack of books.

But then I realized he wouldn't have kept staring if that were actually what I was doing. The flies weren't real.

So I stopped moving altogether. The flies were still there, moving in perfect formation. Maya came back from the copy room a few minutes later and asked me why I was keeping so still. I told her I was studying, but really I was just concentrating on not acting weird. Ian was still watching me.

Then out of nowhere, I felt like I needed to run. Part of me knew it was stupid, but I couldn't help it. I was convinced that I had to run, so I got up and sprinted toward the rows of desks near the reference section and tripped on an uneven piece of carpet and snagged my hand on the edge of a bookcase. It took a pretty big flap of skin off my palm. Enough to look pretty gruesome. Blood gushed all over the floor, and Maya screamed when she saw it. Her face turned white. I think that was the most shocking thing. She screamed in the library. And then started crying.

I'd never seen her cry like that before, like she was scared, and the scary thing is that I liked that she lost control for me. Yes, that makes me a creep and a bad person, but isn't this stupid diary supposed to reflect me as I am? Truthfully? So yeah, I like that she cried because I got hurt. If that makes me a creepy bastard, then that is what I am.

The librarian made a pretty big scene, too, which drew everyone else's attention to the puddle of blood soaking through the carpet.

"I can drive you to the hospital," Ian said, appearing at my side. The librarian looked at him with a soft expression, and I wondered how much of the staff he'd duped into believing that he was a decent human being. How could she miss the hungry expression on his face? That obsessive need for information. Of course he wanted to drive me to the hospital, but there was no way I was going to let *that* happen. Luckily, Maya stepped in just in time so I didn't have to say anything.

"Thanks, but not necessary," Maya said, her cheeks a little pale. "I'll take him."

The librarian's expression indicated that Maya's rejection of Ian's courteous offer was a bit rude, but after assuring her that we'd be able to get to the hospital on our own, we rushed out of the library. I heard people whisper and could feel Ian's eyes on my back as we got out of there. *Douche bag.*

"Why did you start running?" Maya asked, trying to keep her voice calm as she fumbled for her keys.

"Because I'm an idiot," I said, hoping that was a good-enough explanation. She looked at me like it wasn't, but she didn't say anything else as we got into her car. My hand was throbbing.

She had her dad's minivan that day, so she drove me to the emergency room, where we were met by my hysterical mother. Her expression oscillated between concern for me and concern that she might inadvertently say something about my illness in front of Maya.

I told her it was just a cut and that I'd just tripped in the library, but I could feel the questions burning because nobody gets hurt in a library. Seriously.

Once a doctor showed up to stitch up my hand, I sent Maya home. She looked like she wanted to barf, but instead she kissed me, right in front of my mom, and raced out the door without looking back. My mom had the grace to wait until Maya was gone before she whistled.

Paul showed up two seconds later, his lips pursed tight in a thin line. He clapped his hand on my back and had a silent conversation with my mom while the doctor stitched me back together. Paul didn't seem to do well with blood, either. He immediately sat down in a chair near the door and put his head between his knees.

I ordered them both to wait for me outside, and though Mom looked like she wanted to argue, Paul was able to get her out into the hall.

I saw them through the crack in the blinds. They were speaking quickly, a look of pure determination on my mom's face. Then Paul did something I'd never seen him do before. He reached forward and put his hand on my mom's stomach. She stopped talking midsentence when Paul's face split into a wide grin.

They looked happy, and I turned away to watch the doctor finish the last stitch, because it felt like their moment.

Maybe it's time to increase the dosage again.

When we got home, my mom and I had a long talk about what happened and what it might mean. Paul sat quietly, chiming in every so often to offer an opinion or agree with my mom. That's the nice thing about Paul. He knows how to have a serious discussion with someone without putting them down. It's nice to watch him talk to people. I guess that's why he's a good attorney. Anyway, it was decided that we'd talk about increasing my dosage.

I still played tennis with Dwight on Monday. It's my left hand, so I'm fine. He'd already asked me at school how I'd hurt it, but he didn't seem satisfied with any of my answers.

"So tell me again why you were running in the library?" he asked.

"Because I'm an idiot," I said.

"Yes, I know, but seriously," he said.

"I just felt like running."

"In the library?" he asked.

"Yes. In the library." He looked at me funny for a minute and then shrugged. Sometimes I wonder how much Dwight notices about me when we're together. Once in a while I feel like he sees me do something slightly off, but he never says anything. He just lets it slide. Part of me wishes I could tell him. The rest of me thinks that's a bad idea.

You asked what I thought about being a big brother. I haven't had time to really think about the baby as a real person yet. I guess I just hope that the kid doesn't mind that I'm messed up.

DOSAGE: 3 mg. Recommend an increase in dosage.
Not yet approved.

JANUARY 23, 2013

Caaaaan't sleep. Again.

It sucks when you can't sleep. It should be the easiest thing there is. I mean you just have to lie there and let it happen to you, but still it dances just out of reach. It's been like this since I was little, but it got worse when I was diagnosed.

But then, this is a common complaint among my people. We can't sleep, because if we do, the government agents plotting to kill us will slip into our bedrooms and modify the tiny metal chip they're using to track our thoughts.

In my case, the insomnia is a symptom of the drug. Sometimes it makes sleeping feel like a chore, which is a drag because I love to sleep.

Which brings me to the reason I missed school on Monday. Instead of sleeping on Sunday night, I made muffins, cookies, two pies (apple and blueberry), and lemon bars—mostly because my room had been too crowded and noisy. Even Rebecca looked uncomfortable with everyone in there.

The creepy guy with the bowler hat. The birds perched on the edge of my bed. The choir of voices that didn't belong to anyone I could see. I listened for about ten minutes before I couldn't take it anymore. Jason sat in my chair with his feet up on my desk and reminded me to keep quiet so I didn't wake up Paul and my mom. He wasn't really an appealing image with his bare butt cheeks nestled into my furniture, even if he was politely trying to stay out of everyone else's way.

Rebecca followed me to the kitchen, her eyes tired, her face drawn. I pulled out all the baking ingredients while she found a comfortable spot on a stool and watched. I closed all the doors leading to the kitchen and pulled out a whisk. I knew I couldn't use my stand mixer while Mom and Paul were sleeping. Especially if I wanted to avoid awkward questions until morning.

So I baked. I made shortbread cookies to dip in dark chocolate, tiny thumbprint peanut butter cookies, and really complicated little pinwheels with jelly in the center. I was in the zone. I couldn't hear anything except the sound of my spoon scraping the side of the bowl. Blissful silence.

By the time I pulled the second pie out of the oven to cool, my mom was walking downstairs to have breakfast before work. Judging by her expression, I must have looked like hell.

That took some explaining, but honestly, it's probably one of the least-crazy crazy things she's seen me do. She was mad about the mess, which was understandable. There wasn't an inch of counter space that wasn't covered in flour. But rather than yell at me about it, she just started assembling platters of cookies for Paul to take to work. When he walked downstairs and saw the piles of baked goods, he raised an eyebrow to my mom, who shrugged her shoulders and handed him two platters to carry out to his car while she followed him with lemon bars. Paul was actually pretty good about ignoring stuff like this. He says the people in his office like when I bake.

"Leave the blueberry" was the last thing I remember saying. I didn't make it back to my bed. I was more tired than I'd ever been in my life. The kind of tired you feel when you don't know if you're already asleep. And my head was aching. I managed to send Maya a text telling her that I was staying home from school and to "come over later for milk and cookies." I immediately followed this with a text saying, "That's not a euphemism for anything." Though I secretly kind of hoped it was. Also canceled tennis with Dwight.

A few hours later, I staggered to bed, set the phone down on my nightstand, and let the choir sing me back to sleep. Somewhere in the back of my mind, I knew Mom would stay home from work, and for once this didn't bother me. She was cautious and that was okay.

But for the moment, it was just me and Rebecca. She curled up against my chest and fell asleep.

So here I am again in the darkness of my room, with nothing and no one to distract me, and still I can't sleep. I can't stay home tomorrow because I was already out today and I have Academic Team practice. I wouldn't be able to explain it to anyone, even though my mom would understand. So I'm writing to you because I'm so tired I feel drunk. I'm pissed that I can't just doze off like everyone else, but I don't want to take sleeping pills. I don't need more medication.

Maya has been watching me more closely since the library incident, and I seem to be bumping into Ian more frequently at school. He definitely knows there's something wrong with me, so it makes me wonder if he's just waiting for the right moment to do something about it. Also makes me wonder how many other people are starting to notice, too.

Maybe I *should* be taking more pills. Pills for hearing voices. Pills for sleep. Then pills for anxiety about taking too many pills.

Yes, my hand is healing nicely. Thanks for asking.

DOSAGE: 3.5 mg. Increase in dosage approved.

JANUARY 30, 2013

You're slipping.

I expected you to ask that question a long time ago. I mean, it's been months now. What if I'd been dwelling on death all this time and you just now asked me about it?

Anyway, yeah, I used to think about death. Like I said before, my life was a scattered pile of crap when I didn't know if anything was real. I guess for a while I thought about it because death seemed peaceful. More importantly, it seemed quiet. I crave quiet. You have no idea how much time I spend trying to block out the noise in my head.

There's no privacy. Someone is always with you, always watching, always talking about something. When you have a man in a yellow suit asking you what time it is over and over and over again, eventually you want

143

to answer him because you know that is what will send him away. But he's not real. And other people can hear you when you answer his question, so it's hard not to feel frustrated by that. I don't need the attention.

So I didn't think of death as a sad thing. I didn't fear it the way other people do, which isn't necessarily a bad thing. It was only ever bad when I craved it because being me was exhausting. Death seemed like a release that I was too cowardly to reach for because of my family. Even if I could settle on a method that didn't repulse me, I could never have put my mom through the pain of finding my body.

Every day I worried about what I looked like to everyone else and what that would mean for my mom. And I was afraid. Rebecca looked really bad back then.

But I don't think about death anymore. At least not the way I used to. Now I'm more concerned about noticing the ToZaPrex's side effects before anyone else does. But sometimes I miss things, like this week, when something new sprang up.

I didn't know there was a name for it until it started happening more frequently, but it's called tardive dyskinesia. Involuntary muscle movements. It's one of the side effects of the drug—so, yeah, you should probably write that down somewhere and make it official. In my case, it appears to be manifesting itself in grimaces and smacking of lips, which isn't awkward at all. I probably look like a toothless old man eating soup.

I didn't even know I was doing it until Maya stared at me in our religion class and sent me a text: "Why are you frowning like that? Knock it off, you look scary."

It must have looked pretty scary for Maya to text me during class. Sister Catherine has a strict no-cell-phone policy. She confiscates them and hangs them like dead bodies in a bag at the front of the class. But I risked getting caught to text her back: "Bit the inside of my cheek. Ow."

Maya shook her head and turned her attention back to the front of the class. There was sympathy for headaches, a shoulder shrug and a knowing expression that usually meant *This too shall pass.* But there was no sympathy for stupidity. I could almost hear her. *You bit the inside of your cheek? Dumbass.*

But Rebecca, at least, looked sympathetic. She always does.

Sometimes it just takes a little effort to squish my face back into the shape it's supposed to be. I have to focus on the tiny muscles in my cheeks and press my fingers into the skin until the weird flutters of movement stop. It's not so bad. It's easy to pretend I'm just tired.

DOSAGE: 3.5 mg. Same dosage.

FEBRUARY 6, 2013

I'd been asleep for about an hour when Paul opened my door. I could see his silhouette through the hallway light. I could tell he was nervous.

Paul never came into my room. He avoided it completely if he could help it. He'd just poke his head in if he needed something or talk to me from the hallway. I sat upright in bed.

"Your mom is bleeding, and I need to take her to the hospital." The words sort of washed over me as my mom stepped past Paul and through the door.

"Just a little bit. It happened once when I was pregnant with you," she said, touching my face. "We'll be fine. If you need anything, Paul's mom is on standby." She pressed her lips together like she had just eaten a lemon. Her classic *I'm lying to sound brave* expression. Then she kissed me on the cheek.

Paul didn't look convinced. His lips were also pressed together when he nodded, and he met my eyes just once before gently steering my mom toward the garage. Their car pulled out of the driveway almost silently, but I knew Paul was going to floor it the second they pulled out onto the main drag.

The minute they left I realized that I wouldn't be able to sleep. Even if I wanted to, I knew the minute I dozed off, I'd have to deal with the voices. This was probably one of those selfish moments when I shouldn't have been thinking about how hard it was to get back to sleep. I should've been focusing on my mom and Paul and the baby, but those were the things I couldn't control. It never made sense to me to worry about what happened to someone else unless I could help in some way.

And I couldn't help.

It was just past midnight, so I sent Maya a text telling her what was going on. It was kind of shitty of me. She was probably sleeping and I could have woken her up. If not, then she'd be awake reading and I'm bothering her with something she can't fix, either. But I ended the text with: So I'm texting you because I can't sleep.

There was no response, so once again I was wide

awake and alone. I recited some of my favorite lines in my head. The Saint Crispin's Day speech. The warning in front of Gringotts Bank.

So I closed my eyes and waited for the sound of Mom and Paul's car. I knew it wouldn't happen for hours, but I needed something to focus on and I didn't really want to give up on sleep. If I turned on the TV, I would have absolutely no chance of dozing off at all. If I opened a book or the blinds, I might get distracted by something. If I started baking now, I'd never stop, and my mom would never leave me alone in the house again. Paul's mom would move in with us, and that would be the end of my life.

I was starting to think about my new little brother or sister, and my insides had started to go cold when my window opened of its own volition and a pair of legs stepped through. I pulled the blanket back up to my throat and waited. My nighttime visitors had never been real before, and my bedroom is on the second floor, so it was unlikely that someone had climbed the lattice leaning against the house, but when I heard the visitor speak, I doubted myself.

"Adam?" she asked in the darkness.

"Maya, what are you doing here?" I whispered.

"Being rebellious," she said, and I could tell even in the dark that she was smiling.

Without warning, she kicked off her shoes and slipped into bed with me. My whole body went rigid when she threw her arm over my chest.

"You said you couldn't sleep," she said.

"And you thought you'd come help?"

"Nope."

She kissed me and everything sort of went fuzzy.

With one leg on either side of my body she reached down to tangle her fingers in my hair. Maya was not this girl. She was not the girl who climbed through her boyfriend's window for some midnight fondling. It wasn't her. And I knew better than to assume that my mind wasn't playing tricks on me. It seemed more likely that Maya was in her room, sleeping in her own bed. So while she was kissing me, I reached over her shoulder for my phone and sent her a text that said "Hi."

The tiny buzzing in her pocket was the most welcome sound I've ever heard in my life. How else was I supposed to tell if she was real?

She pulled out her phone and raised an eyebrow.

"Did you seriously just text me while we're making out?" And of course I didn't have an answer that didn't sound crazy.

"Maybe," I said.

"Idiot," she whispered, and she latched her lips back onto mine.

We kissed for a while, hours maybe. My hands went everywhere, and for a few blissful moments, it felt like nothing was off limits. They drifted over her stomach and then lingered on her breasts. She breathed in deeply but didn't stop me.

I've never really understood the preoccupation with the size of a girl's breasts. I mean, yes, we are drawn to an ample bosom the same way other primates are drawn to brilliantly colored hindquarters, but as my fingertips traveled over Maya's nipples, it didn't matter that her breasts were small. It didn't make me want them less, and I could feel her heart race when I circled them with my fingers, tracing the curve.

It was early Saturday morning. She wouldn't be missed until her brothers woke up, and that wouldn't be for a few more hours. So I did what any guy would do in my situation. I searched for the line. The invisible line that all girls draw around them that governs where they will allow someone to touch them.

I found it at the elastic band of her underwear. I thought for a moment that she was going to jump out of my bed and out the window, but she just redirected my hands somewhere else. A gentle *Not yet*. I got the message.

Eventually, we had to stop. Not because either of us wanted to (since I wasn't exactly in a hurry to end the best night of my life), but her parents would notice if she wasn't at home, and mine would notice if I had a guest in my room when they got back.

"They're going to be fine," she said simply, nestling into my chest. I nodded. She'd come over to distract me and it'd worked. When she finally climbed out the window (which we both later agreed was completely unnecessary because my mom and Paul were gone), I stayed in bed just thinking. But the thoughts were sharp and painful, so I thought about Maya instead. My perfect, neurotic girlfriend who can get away with anything because no one expects her to do anything wrong.

Mom and Paul got home around ten-thirty in the morning. Everything was fine, just like Maya said it would be. Paul touched my shoulder in what he considered an affectionate sort of way, which I accepted. Mom kissed me on the top of my head before heading off to bed to sleep for a while.

Then, and again I don't know why I feel this compulsion to tell you this or anything for that matter, I went to my room and cried because I felt guilty for being selfish. For wanting to distract myself from what was happening to my mom.

Maya sent me a text later: "Keep your window unlocked."

I heard a train whistle.

My mom told me something once, right after my dad left. You lose your secrets when you let people get too close. That was the scariest thing for her when she started dating.

I get it now. It's hard to let someone find you in all the dark and twisty places inside, but eventually, you have to hope that they do, because that's the beginning of everything.

It's ridiculous that you would ask me why I haven't told Maya. You know me now, better than almost anyone. Even though you can't tell me what my voice sounds like, you read every word I write and talk to me for an hour every week. During that hour, you tell me stories about your life—or you make them up. It didn't occur to me until just now that everything you've told me might be a lie based on your need to connect with me, even though you can't fix me.

Maybe that's the Harvard kid in you, trying to prove yourself or trying not to be a failure. I get that. You must have been under a lot of pressure to perform at school. From your plethora of diplomas, I can tell that you are a junior, meaning that someone thought it would be a good idea to name you after your father. I've never been a fan of that.

Naming someone after someone else is a huge

responsibility. What if you'd turned out to be a drug-addled teenager? But of course that didn't happen. Maybe in this case the name forced you to behave, but just so you know, any kid named Winston Xavier Edmonton III is basically asking to get their ass kicked. So if you did do this to one of your kids and they happen to come home one day with a black eye, that's on you.

But that's what people do to their kids, I guess. They give them a name and then expect that they'll grow into it eventually, never suspecting that it might never fit. Because it sucks to disappoint your parents. There's nothing more gut-wrenching than looking into their eyes and seeing that you're not what they expected.

I'm not afraid of telling Maya about me. At least not in the same way I'm afraid of losing control. It's just not something I want to think about too much. I want to keep her far enough away so she won't ever have to see me as I actually am. I don't want to lose my secrets, because they keep me safe. The world can see what I choose to show it, because I am lucky enough to hide behind this drug. This miraculous, life-altering drug that has given me my strength back and protected me from myself. Funny when you have to take medicine to protect you from yourself, isn't it?

I guess I just don't want her to know the truth. I'm afraid of what she'd do with that information.

I doubt she'd ever climb through my window again. She might even be afraid to be alone with me. It might ruin the way she looks at me with her side smile, the one that secretly makes me feel like I'm waking up on the first day of summer vacation. I don't even care how cheesy that sounds. And I don't care how much time I have to waste in your office before you realize how useless this is.

I'd really just like to keep my secrets for a while.

I can always tell when my mom has gotten in your head. The questions are more direct.

Yes. I was uncomfortable at the latest ultrasound appointment. Paul would probably have been okay with leaving me out of it, but he was a good sport for my mom's sake, as usual.

Let's examine the situation for a second. For once, my discomfort has nothing to do with my illness. Not a goddamned thing.

Any sixteen-year-old would want to barf upon seeing their heavily pregnant mother bare her gigantic belly as a doctor covers it with lube. My reaction (disgust) was not unnatural. My mom was lying on a table, half naked, while Paul erotically rubbed her shoulders and every so often whispered something in her ear. Then she blushed. Honestly, I don't need to see that, hear that, or be within five hundred feet of that happening. The touching alone is really not something I need to witness. If her swollen stomach wasn't enough of an indicator, I already know that my mom is sexually active. And as her teenage son, I think I have done a really spectacular job of being okay with that.

I am glad they're happy. It's great my mom won't need to work when the baby is born because this time she can afford to stay home if she wants. Yes, I'm being sincere. I get that everything happening in her life is a tremendous blessing, and she deserves every ounce of happiness. Even the nauseating, cutesy, romantic bullshit she and Paul are so good at.

But Jesus Christ. I did not need to hear about my mom's uterine walls. I didn't need to know that having sex is a healthy way to induce labor when the time comes. I didn't need to watch Paul's hand travel up and down my mom's belly. I may never be able to unsee that. In fact, I'm pretty sure the images are burned into my eyelids. None of those moments were necessary for me.

And you know the scariest part of the whole experience? When the doctor started talking about breastfeeding, my nipples started to hurt. *My* nipples.

My nipples will never do an honest day's work in their lives, and yet they were concerned enough about my future brother or sister to burn with discomfort the moment someone else mentioned breastfeeding. I actually have a diagnosed mental condition that bothers me less than the fact that I have empathetic nipples. I don't even know if anything can be done about this, but I would genuinely like to believe that my areolas will go back to being decoration.

And I know by the way you ask "How do you feel?" that my mom is actually the one asking. She wants to know how I feel about the baby. It was her intention to make the doctor's appointment something we could all do together. I'm sure it looked more picturesque in her head. Everyone all smiley and gathered together around her belly.

There was a moment that I liked, though. I got to hear the baby's heartbeat. The steady *womp womp womp womp* of blood pumping in and out of a tiny life that has no idea we're all watching it on the screen. We all sort of froze. My mom cried. Paul sort of teared up, and somewhere in the corner of the room behind the curtains, Rebecca was sobbing into her dress.

When I told Maya about the heartbeat later, she squeezed my hand. I don't know why.

DOSAGE: 4 mg. Increased dosage.

FEBRUARY 13, 2013

You don't ask that many questions about my other doctors. The ones on the panel for the drug study. I think you probably avoid asking questions about them because you don't want to remind me that this drug is still experimental and the only reason I am taking it is because Paul has a doctor friend who knew about the research and was able to get me into the study. Or maybe you don't like the thought of me seeing the other doctors because you think we have something special and you'd hate to see me happily medicated with someone else, you sick bastard. After everything we've been through together, you're afraid I'd leave you for someone younger and prettier.

I'll put your mind at ease. The doctors on the study panel are all old. But they do have a ton of young interns. Yeah, I see the other participants in the halls sometimes when my mom takes me in, but it's not exactly a place where I want to make friends. I know you said it might be beneficial to talk to people who are going through the same stuff I am, but I don't see that as helpful. I don't want to talk to other people like me. I can't help them. I'm crazy, too.

The doctors ask me everything from the ever-popular "How do you feel?" to the awkward "Does the drug seem to be causing any sexual complications for you?"

"I am not having sex."

"With masturbation?"

"No. That works fine."

"Excellent."

Yeah, it's nice to know that even on the drug I can masturbate properly. The doctors seemed gratified to learn this as well.

They were pleased with all the results, actually. Since I'd been such a whack job to begin with, they were glad that the drug had completely transformed me, allowing me to live a relatively normal life. They congratulated themselves a lot on the success of the drug, the success of the study, and their overall brilliance. I was okay with it because it was benefiting me, but after a while, they *did* sound like douche bags. The thing about being smart is that you don't actually need to remind people you're smart every five seconds. It makes people want to kill you.

I know that experimental treatments are for the ones who have no other options. You know about the incident that got me enrolled in the study, of course. It's all in my file.

You've got to understand that I was sick. Not just the regular kind of schizo-sick-in-the-head. I had a fever. I was burning up. Little puddles of sweat had formed in my eye sockets, and I could feel the moisture weighing down my lids. I remember feeling disoriented, like I'd suddenly lost my balance. That was when I saw it slither underneath the kitchen cabinets. A thick green snake that I thought had come in from the backyard. I leaped onto the table.

I grabbed my mom's kitchen scissors and stabbed at it as its tail whipped back and forth, slapping the tile. It lunged, and I brought the scissors down on what I thought was its body.

My mom found me in a pool of my own blood, the handles of the scissors jutting out of my thigh. I don't even remember doing it. Sometimes I think I can remember the blinding pain and the loud crack of my head hitting the ground, but then I remember the snake, too. So I don't trust my memory.

That was after they'd taken me out of school. When I spent almost six months in my house, unable to do anything and not wanting to move. Rebecca didn't smile back then. She definitely didn't twirl. We just sort of covered ourselves in blankets and watched reruns of *Avatar: The Last Airbender.*

I had really awful reactions to the first few drugs they tried. One of them actually landed me in the hospital with chest pain, so I was pretty sure I'd never be able to live my life. I was angry all the time. Usually I did what the voices told me to do because I just wanted them to stop. I wanted it to end, and I knew the fastest way to make that happen was to just do it. Slap my own face. Pinch my skin. Run and don't stop running.

Is it weird that I think part of me will never stop running?

Ah yes, the baby. At five months it should be about ten inches long. It can hear our voices now, so my mom makes a big deal about everyone talking to her belly. Paul and I take turns doing this. Because we love her.

It's actually a testament to our love that neither of us said a word when she burst into tears because her feet were too fat for her slippers, even though her voice got really high and squeaky and we probably could've laughed about it.

Last night, before dinner, my voices were singing to me. I actually like it when they do that because it's a nice break from them telling me that my family would be better off if I killed myself. They weren't singing any words that I recognized, but I hummed along for a while until the tune sort of floated out of me. I didn't notice my mom step through the doorway while I was doing this, but when I looked up, she was smiling, her hands clasped over her belly. She said the baby liked my voice. I didn't argue with her.

Yes, of course I have something planned for Valentine's Day. It's tomorrow. Do you have something planned? You're the one married with three kids. It's almost expected that I am going to do something because Maya and I are young and stupid and can celebrate this holiday by watching a crappy movie, eating a crappy dinner, and ending the evening with inappropriate touching.

I'm not sure why it's relevant to you if I have a physical relationship with my girlfriend. Maybe you get off thinking about it. I wouldn't be surprised. You seem like the type to have weird fetishes like that, but to answer your question, no, we have not had sex. We have done everything else, though, which makes us far from innocent, I can assure you. And it usually happens during Academic Team matches.

Since she doesn't know I go to therapy every Wednesday, she doesn't have to know what I tell you. In fact, it's better that she has no idea what we talk about. It can stay between us. There's no reason for me to feel guilty about writing this to you, but even as I write this, I feel Rebecca cringe. She doesn't like secrets, but she also really doesn't like it when I talk about Maya. It makes her feel uncomfortable, like it's a betrayal of trust or something. But here's the thing: I feel guilty sometimes about not talking to you.

The least I can do is be completely honest here. This is still my free space, where I can write anything that comes to mind, anything that needs to be evaluated. It's nice having a place to work this stuff out.

But you don't care about that. You want to know what I do with my girlfriend and how it makes me *feel*. Every damn time. *And how do you feel today, Adam?* I have to give you credit for continuing to ask the same question and continuing to wait for a verbal response. You are stubborn. But you know what? I think it would be better if everyone in the entire world stopped asking people how they feel and starting talking about what they *think*. Nobody gives a shit about feelings. They are useless, pathetic wastes of time for believers in astrology and unicorns.

I think that touching Maya is unlike anything I've ever done. When the seniors compete in their Academic Team match, we usually sneak out. Everyone knows what we're doing, but nobody says anything. It's like an unspoken code. Sometimes we go to the football field, or sometimes the basketball courts. High school campuses are great places to make out when no one is there. The hidden spaces are endless. I wonder if people think about that when designing them.

I've learned all the ways she likes to be kissed, and I've mastered the appropriate amount of tongue, which was not as easy as I thought it would be. Adding tongue to kissing is delicate business. I wasn't sure how to do it until I felt hers in my mouth, slowly examining my tongue, then retreating back into her mouth, inviting me in.

The kisses on the neck seemed to get an immediate response, but here's something I didn't know—it's the ears that drive her crazy. Gentle nibbling. Nothing too aggressive. *Lightly.* It almost feels better to know that she likes something than to have her do something I like. At some point, she always stops me, then we have to wait until I can stand again.

When we get back to the match, no one asks about where we'd been. Turns out, Dwight has even been making excuses for us with Sister Helen.

He's a good guy.

DOSAGE: 4.5 mg. Increased dosage.

FEBRUARY 20, 2013

St. Agatha's choir raises money for their DC trip by charging $5 for a singing telegram on Valentine's Day. This means that class came to a screeching halt every time they burst into our classroom. Rebecca loved it. She danced along to the music as if nothing could possibly be more glorious. Meanwhile, Jason stood next to me and kept muttering, *Be cool, try smiling. I know this is lame, but try not to look like such an angry giant.*

Both Marys got a telegram in English. Rosa from Academic Team got one in biology from her boyfriend on the cross-country team. Clare got one from her secret admirer, which was Dwight because he told me he was going to do it and wanted to know how lame that was on a scale of one to ten.

Seven, I told him.

I asked Maya if it would make me a bad boyfriend if I didn't send her a singing telegram for Valentine's Day.

"Please don't," she said seriously. "I'll die."

I laughed and agreed not to. We spent the rest of the morning watching the parade of red and pink balloons wander the halls between classes, and I gave her the heart-shaped cookies I'd baked her, which turned out to be so much better than the telegram. Her words, not mine.

Ian happened to be walking through the hallway at the same time. He saw the cookies and said, "Are those an apology because you're too cheap to get her an actual gift?"

I was going to respond when Maya kissed me pointedly, and inappropriately, in the middle of the hallway, causing people to whistle and catcall. She raised an eyebrow at Ian and pulled me into class.

"Nicely done," I said.

"I know," said Maya.

In honor of Valentine's Day, Sister Catherine made a big deal about discussing chastity and the virtues of saving yourself for marriage. She did this while one of the Marys in the front row scratched unconsciously at the birth control patch on her back. Don't ask me how I know this.

There are, of course, the religious types whose parents have convinced them that sex is a nasty invention of the morally depraved, whose only unsavory purpose is to create tiny, mucus-covered infants. But they're weirdos, and everyone knows it.

I'd like to tell you that my Valentine's Day went by without incident, but I guess stuff is starting to slip through the cracks. Either the dose is too low or my body has gotten too used to it. That can happen, right? Either way, something feels off, and I could feel myself losing control fairly early in the night.

It's not like Maya and I had never been on a date before. We've had meals together and gone places together and done all the things most couples would label "date-like" activities, but I guess there's something about Valentine's Day that makes it official. No amount of late-night study sessions and fondling can replace the sight of two other couples from school seeing you out with your girlfriend. It's a rite of passage.

Maya drove. I had a headache when I got in the car but didn't say anything. She looked beautiful. Like, really beautiful. Something about the way she was smiling. She didn't seem worried about anything. And she was wearing blue. I like her in blue.

She was the kind of beautiful that makes other guys jealous. There's something kind of awesome about having something that other people want. That's messed up, I know, but that isn't the only reason I was glad she looked so great. It was nice that the rest of the world got to see her that way.

"So it's our first Valentine's Day," she said after we sat down at our table. "Is this the part where we stare into each other's eyes and say what we like about each other?"

"That sounds pretty lame," I said. "How about we stare into each other's eyes and say what we *know* about each other. A recap, if you will."

She laughed, scooted her chair closer, and fixed me with a laser-focused stare. "Okay, you start," she said.

"You still can't swim."

"I can too! I took the lessons you got me! At least now I won't drown."

"I doubt you'll get arm floaties when the ice caps melt, Maya."

"Well, you're a really slow runner." She grinned.

It went on for a while. This picking on each other. Completely inappropriate for Valentine's Day, but we couldn't stop laughing.

She bites her nails. I don't walk straight. She hates bananas. I can't pronounce Spanish words. She's afraid of hippos. I love Star Wars.

"You're a lot sweeter than you look," she said.

"What's that supposed to mean?" I asked playfully, eyebrows raised, with my mouth full of ravioli.

"I don't mean it like that. It's just that some people

might be intimidated by you because you're so big and you look kind of stern sometimes. But you're kind. And actually really thoughtful."

"Thanks," I said, pretending to blush. "How do I look stern?"

"You get headaches a lot more than you should," she said finally. "I think they make you a little twitchy." I thought about this for a second and nodded.

"And you notice things that other people don't," I said.

Actually, Maya's perceptiveness is really inconvenient. It's gotten a lot harder to hide things from her, and I don't want her to dig any deeper into my headaches or "twitchiness." I'll have to start making a bigger effort to distract her from that.

So we finished dinner and even managed to catch a sunset by the beach, which I thought was cliché but she seemed to like. It was when we got to the theater playing black-and-white movies that I really started feeling sick. It was one of those old theaters with burgundy plush-cushioned seats. There weren't that many people there, which was good because it wasn't stadium seating. Meaning that I would easily block the view of anyone sitting behind me.

Rebecca, who had been conspicuously absent all day, was sitting three rows ahead of us. When she looked back, she seemed worried. My pulse quickened and I took Maya's hand. I was not going to ruin Valentine's Day for her. I was going to be her normal boyfriend. The kind who holds her hand and tells her she looks beautiful. For a little while, I was able to be that guy.

We were watching *Casablanca*. When I'd planned the date, I thought it would be a good idea to watch something both of us had already seen. No need to pay attention.

The sound was a half second behind the picture, which was doing weird things to my head, but there were a few minutes when I thought I could watch the movie like everyone else, until I felt that familiar tug at the back of my brain. The tiny piece of me that wants to believe everything I see took control.

It was at the part when Ilsa enters the nightclub and asks the guy at the piano to play "As Time Goes By," knowing that it would get Rick's attention. The room of crowded people was hard to watch. Everyone was doing something different. Drinking. Talking. It was hard to focus on what was going on and not lose the story.

That was when I noticed that the people on-screen had started to merge into the theater. None of them were staying put on the screen. They sank into the audience, and I jumped a little when the German soldiers burst into the club.

"Are you okay?" Maya asked.

"I'm fine," I lied.

For another ten minutes, I moved between varying degrees of panic. I was losing it. Rebecca had started to cry. Neither of us could control what was happening. Then somewhere in the movie, guns started going off and tiny shards of glass fell from the ceiling. Whatever shield I had been using to hide my crazy disappeared. I leaned over, yanked Maya to the ground, and protected her from the bullets I thought were blasting through the theater.

I cupped her body gently so she didn't hit the ground too hard. My elbows got the brunt of the fall. I really *did* believe the bullets were flying, and I was crying a little because I thought I wouldn't be able to save her. The top half of her body fit neatly into the curve of my arm, and once we hit the sticky movie theater floor, she looked up at me for a second in shock.

She started kissing me. I couldn't understand what was happening. Somewhere in the back of my mind, I noticed that the couples who had been sitting in our row had moved somewhere else when I launched my girlfriend from her seat and dragged her to the floor. But Maya was kissing me like I *hadn't* just done something completely irrational. Or maybe she was kissing me because I *had* done something completely irrational. And if that was the case, should I have been worried about her? No, really, I'm asking you. This is what we pay you for.

The only real thing in the world was her lips. She was

kissing me and running her fingers through my hair. Maybe she thought I was sexy?

The rest of the people in the theater might have kept watching *Casablanca*. I could still hear the movie going. I'll never know, though, because I was on the disgusting movie theater floor, making out with my girlfriend.

We didn't get up when the movie ended. The guy who comes around and sweeps up the popcorn found us and told us we had to leave so they could let people in for the next show. We weren't even embarrassed.

I feel fine now. I'm not disoriented anymore. I guess it was just a passing thing.

When I replay the events of that night with a clear head, I can see that I must not have tugged Maya to the ground that hard. I must not have looked as outwardly afraid as I felt inside. I probably wasn't crying. Maybe I just teared up. We must have looked like two teenagers who really wanted to make out on Valentine's Day instead of watch a movie we've both seen before.

I know how this sounds. I've written this whole thing down several times, and I still can't find anything that needs to be changed. The details seem correct, and even though I can anticipate your questions, answering them seems boring. I might have had a momentary lapse of judgment. It's entirely possible that my mind played images that had absolutely nothing to do with what I actually did.

But sometimes the things that happen aren't as important as the things you remember. Maya looked beautiful. We had a relatively normal Valentine's Day dinner followed by normal Valentine's Day activities that did not lead to sex. I wasn't even that crushed by that.

I remember kissing her in the minivan for a long time, until my lips hurt. She dropped me off at my house, and I walked through the front door to find Paul working on his laptop.

He asked how the date was. I told him it was good. He looked like he'd been waiting up for me. He cracked his knuckles again like he did when he was forcing conversation.

"Yes?" I asked.

Paul looked up at me like he was going to lay an egg. He had something to say that he didn't want to say. Like, *really* didn't want to say. It looked painful for him when he actually spoke.

"In your bathroom, behind the toilet paper, there's a box of condoms."

We both looked at each other. He nodded. Then I nodded. And I knew we would never talk about it again.

But I laughed when I got back to my room. I appreciated the gesture, but I have been walking around with a condom in my wallet for over a month. I will be ready when Maya is.

DOSAGE: 4.5 mg. Same dosage.

FEBRUARY 27, 2013

Awesome. Just awesome.

I got picked to play Jesus for the junior class's rendition of the Stations of the Cross for Easter. This is basically the worst thing that's ever happened to me at this school.

Kids vote on who plays Jesus, Mary Magdalene, Veronica, and Mary, Jesus's mother. It's highly political. No one ever wants to do it, so people sort of gang up on other, less popular people and get them to do the big roles with the majority of the speaking lines, leaving the highly coveted crowd-member positions wide open.

I'm pretty sure that Ian had something to do with my campaign for Jesus, though, because I'm actually not detested at school.

Dwight managed to snag a narrator spot, which is the

next-best thing to crowd member, where all you have to do is say "Crucify him!" at the right time.

"How did you manage that?" I asked him.

"I volunteered."

"Why the hell didn't you tell me to volunteer for something?" I asked.

"It's every man for himself, dude."

That rat bastard. He could've told me. He could've told me to volunteer for something else. Instead he just said, "Jesus, though . . . Man, that sucks."

The worst thing is that I am taller than the plywood cross they usually use.

Therefore, not only am I quiet, secretly schizophrenic Jesus, I am also Giant Jesus. Giant, Arms-Wide-Open, Rio de Janeiro Jesus.

They have to find me a bigger cross. During our very first run-through, I looked absolutely ridiculous carrying over my shoulder a tiny cross that didn't even touch the ground. I would've had to squat to be nailed to it. It's the only time I've ever seen Maya laugh in church. To her credit, she was laughing with me and not at me, like the rest of them. I think.

She didn't get off easy, though. She's Mary Magdalene, which is highly amusing and makes me think that my classmates are actually smarter than they look.

St. Agatha's does not take its Stations of the Cross

lightly. Every class has to do its own performance, and Maya says they are almost always the same. Girls basically all wear a blue sheet over their uniforms, while boys borrow altar boy robes, and sometimes (if they are really into it) they get fake beards.

When I was chosen, Sister Catherine seemed anxious about it, like she wasn't sure that it was such a good idea for me to be on display in the middle of church, but she said nothing. She didn't even talk to my mom about it, which I thought was odd, given the circumstances, but didn't question it because for once no one was calling me crazy. After all, I am supposed to be the Lamb of God, here to remove the sins of the world.

"Adam, how do you think Jesus would feel at this moment?" Sister Catherine asked seriously.

Be nice, Jason advised, appearing out of nowhere. I tried to avert my gaze from his blindingly white butt cheeks as he strolled down the row of pews, but it was impossible.

I looked at the robe I was wearing and tugged at the fake crown of thorns, which actually did itch like hell, and wanted to respond to Sister Catherine sarcastically, but was saved from having to say anything when someone farted and the crowd immediately dispersed. Jason had already vanished.

It's actually kind of fascinating. There aren't many

school performances that focus on the murder of the main character. The whole story is about my slow and painful demise, like a parade of inhuman suffering that keeps Catholics coming back for more.

Come see the junior class's production of the Stations of the Cross. Watch Jesus die. Again.

I'm not one to beg for popularity, but if I had been just a little bit more likable, I probably could've gotten a sweet gig as a Roman soldier.

Maya came over later to watch me bake cookies. Before you ask, yes, we *do* go out, but for the most part we just hang out.

She never asks questions about baking, which I think is odd because she's curious about everything else.

"Do you want me to teach you how to bake?" I asked.

"No," she said a little too quickly.

"Why not?" I asked. It was unlike her to avoid learning something for herself.

"Cookies don't require any thought if all you're doing is eating them, but they require a certain degree of *thoughtfulness* if you make them for someone," she said.

I could've argued, but I didn't want to take that away from her. Sometimes you just want to enjoy someone handing you a plate of cookies.

DOSAGE: 4.5 mg. Same dosage.

MARCH 6, 2013

At some point, Dwight and I probably could've stopped meeting up on Monday nights and our moms would have been appeased. But we're creatures of habit, so we kept it up.

And Dwight is actually pretty laid-back. Even though he talks nonstop, he doesn't really go out of his way to make friends at school. It makes me wonder how he'd react if he knew everything about me. Not that I'm stupid enough to tell him.

Somehow our dads came up in conversation when I told him about my mom and stepdad.

"Dad left when I was eight," I told him.

Dwight pondered this for a moment. "My mom was artificially inseminated," he said.

There's really no response to that. I think I stared

at him blankly until he said something about his mom being too busy with her career to devote any time to dating, but I'm not sure if that was just what she told Dwight.

If I had wanted to mention anything personal about my own life, that would have been the moment to do it.

There's definitely a divide between the people in my life who know everything about me and the people who don't. It's probably unhealthy to create that between the people I spend most of my time with. It probably means I'm trying to compartmentalize my crazy.

I overheard Paul on the phone with his mom the other day. Most people would say she's a nice old lady. The kind who always has hard candies and would never dream of showing up at a party empty-handed. But she's very comfortable with words like "Oriental" and "colored" at home, and whispers the word "Mexican" when we go out to eat. Nobody bothers to tell her that "Mexican" isn't a dirty word.

Like I said, she seems nice, but she's not. She doesn't trust me. She said as much when she asked me if I could let her know when I was starting to lose control so she could do something. She pulled a can of pepper spray out of her purse and shook it at me. What the hell, lady? No, not to get an ambulance or alert someone to the fact that I was having an episode due to my debilitating mental condition. That bitch wanted to *pepper spray me in the face*. I didn't tell my mom because she has a hard-enough time putting up with Paul's mom in small doses. If she found out she'd said something like that to me, it would just make things worse.

When my mom got pregnant, Paul's mom started calling more often. It was usually on Paul's cell, but once in a while it was the house line. We must be the only family that doesn't use caller ID, and my mom pays dearly for it every time her mother-in-law calls to give her un-wanted advice about the baby. Like about how if it's a boy, she has to have him circumcised, which she knows my mom is vehemently against. And yes, she was against it when I was born, too. So now you actually do know more about me than you ever wanted to know.

Anyway, I overheard Paul on the phone with his mom the other day and knew they were talking about me. To Paul's credit, he actually didn't say anything that wasn't true. I overheard: "Yes, we've got it under control. No, Mother, I am not underestimating anything, and if you accuse me of not taking my child's safety seriously again, I'm going to get very angry with you. Love you. Bye."

Paul ends every phone call with family members with "Love you."

No matter how heated the argument is. He could have had a conversation like: *I HATE YOU AND I HOPE YOU*

REALIZE HOW MUCH SHAME AND DISHONOR YOU'VE BROUGHT ON THE FAMILY. . . . Love you.

Since I can't talk to Maya about *this* stuff, the business of being crazy, I talk to her about other, related issues, like the baby. The problem is that Maya has a pretty easy time ignoring me when she's studying. She hears everything I'm saying, somewhere in the back of her perfectly cataloged mind, but she will not let anything ruin her concentration until she is finished with her thought. She can sit for hours with a notebook in perfect silence without letting anything interrupt her.

She's trained herself to do this because she wants to be a doctor someday. Not a doctor who sees patients. A researcher. She doesn't like people, and she definitely doesn't like dealing with their problems on a human level. And yes, before you ask, that is something that I've known for a while. Maya likes "person." Singular. People in a group basically suck.

With the help of my medication, I can hide my problems from her. Well, the big one. If she thinks it's weird that I have chronic headaches and insomnia, she doesn't say anything. Those things on their own don't point to what I have.

She's empathetic when she wants to be, but she does it in her own Maya-ish way: by pointing out a problem and then agreeing with you that, yes, it does in fact suck balls. Like when we were talking about the baby after Academic Team practice.

"There's always going to be this huge difference between the way the first kid was raised and the way the next one is raised," she said. "Since you have different dads and a gigantic age gap between you, it'll be huge. I mean, you could potentially be another father figure for this kid. You should also be prepared for the fact that they will get away with pretty much everything. If you weren't allowed to do something as a child, chances are Baby 2.0 will get away with it, no problem." She took her glasses off and looked at me very seriously. "When I was little, I had a chore wheel. My mom would put things on the chore wheel that I had to do or I wouldn't be able to watch TV or have dessert. When my brothers were born, the chore wheel was abolished. There were two of them, so my parents abandoned all previously established codes of conduct because the main things became keeping them clean and fed.

"It took a long time to potty train them. They are almost six now, and they still have accidents. The bathroom I share with them never smells right. The trash can in there is regularly filled with dirty underwear. My mom literally rewards them for not shitting their pants. Practically throws them a parade for not shitting their pants.

"That is what you have to look forward to, Adam.

They get rewarded for not shitting their pants. It's best that you just accept this now. It'll make things easier."

So, yeah, that was really helpful nonadvice.

We had our final Academic Team match on Tuesday after school. Dwight was in rare form, Maya solved a pretty complicated equation, and I was happily benched. No hallucinations.

At the end of the match, we all sat around while some seniors packed up the game equipment and folded the chairs. Clare and Rosa were talking about prom coming up in May, while Maya and Dwight argued about some homework problem I'd stopped paying attention to about five minutes earlier. My friends talk about boring shit sometimes.

In the middle of their argument, Maya absentmindedly put her hand on my thigh. No one else noticed. It was natural and completely innocent, but something about the way she did it . . . felt good. Like I was being claimed. And I guess you're not supposed to want to be claimed by someone, but I really don't care. I'm her person.

Yep, I feel fine.

DOSAGE: 5 mg. Increased dosage.

MARCH 13, 2013

Doc, I should start this by saying you've looked really tired these past couple of weeks. I don't know what's going on at home or if my therapy sessions have become more exhausting for you than normal, but you should really get some sleep. Your eyes are all bloodshot and you look like hell. I assume that you already know what the other doctors said. The tests were inconclusive, so they're running them again, but they've basically told us that the drug might be doing more damage than good:

"Adam, we've been monitoring your vitals and making note of any radical changes, and unfortunately, though there were positive signs to begin with, it does not appear that you will be a good candidate for this treatment long term. It would be detrimental to the study to continue using your data, because even though you have not reverted to your previous state, you have already exhibited signs of resistance to the drug. We will begin tapering you off to lower doses."

It was sort of harsh the way they told me about it. "Detrimental to the study"—like I was a lab rat. They didn't tell me this the way they'd tell a patient with cancer that chemo isn't going to work, because cancer is sexy. I don't mean that it's better than schizophrenia or that people who have it are sexier than people who have anything else. Or that cancer is actually sexy. Obviously. I mean that cancer patients don't frighten anyone. When you have cancer, people are sympathetic. They feel something for you, and people even hold races to raise money for your cure.

It's different when people are afraid of what you've got, because then you get some of the sympathy but none of the support. They don't wish you ill—they just want you as far away from them as possible.

Cancer Kid has the Make-A-Wish Foundation because Cancer Kid will eventually die, and that's sad. Schizophrenia Kid will also eventually die, but before he does, he will be overmedicated with a plethora of drugs, he will alienate everyone he's ever really cared about, and he will most likely wind up on the street, living with a cat that will eat him when he dies. That is also sad, but nobody gives him a wish, because he isn't actively dying.

It is abundantly clear that we only care about sick people who are dying tragic, time-sensitive deaths.

I got nervous when the doctors told me they might take me off the drug. Mom says they aren't going to do anything hasty and we're still going to find a medication that does everything I need it to do, but I think she was just trying to keep me calm. She was trying to say the things she knew would make me feel better, because that's what moms do, but I was still nervous, and sometimes when I get nervous, I try to do things that aren't always a good idea.

It started with the weird skin around my cuticle, the stuff that looks like frayed pieces of string cheese. I pulled at it. When I saw red flesh and the blood underneath, I kept going because it was the kind of pain that felt satisfying. Like the time I pulled out three baby teeth when they weren't even loose because it felt good to pull them. I mean, it hurt, but in a good way, like the way sucking a canker sore feels good.

So I pulled the cuticle skin up to my first knuckle. That was when I stopped because I was bleeding a lot, and I knew I wouldn't be able to hide anything worse than that. My mom would know I'd done something if I had anything more than one Band-Aid on my finger. She always knew when there was something off, even if she can't always remember where she left her cell phone. A

Band-Aid wouldn't draw attention. It wouldn't make me lose my kitchen knife privileges.

I'm not sure it was just the possibility of being taken off the drug that made me nervous. I'd also seen someone at the grocery store a few days ago. Someone I hadn't seen in more than a year.

Remember Todd? The old best friend I told you about? He lives a few streets over from my house, and in kindergarten we both had the same Batman lunch box. We used to ride our bikes together.

Back when I was first diagnosed a year and a half ago, I told him everything. For a few days after that, he was still my best friend. He didn't act like anything was different. Then my mom got a call from his mom. I couldn't tell what his mom was saying, but my mom was using language I couldn't believe. She listened to Todd's mom for a few seconds and then said, "He is nothing to be afraid of." Her words came out of her like a low, dangerous hiss, and when she hung up, she was shaking. I was in the hall when this happened, just watching her through a crack in the door. We didn't talk about it after it happened. I just suddenly understood that I wouldn't be seeing Todd anymore.

But anyway, there he was in the grocery store. I didn't notice him at first; Rebecca did. I just sort of followed her gaze to where he was standing next to the breakfast foods. He was twirling the keys to his mom's Acura around his finger in a distracted sort of way while he looked at cereal, so that meant he already had his license and he was running errands. He pretty much looked the same. He'd started growing a beard. If we were still friends, I would've told him it looked like his chin was growing mold, but we weren't, so I didn't.

He was wearing a weird anime T-shirt from some obscure Japanese cartoon, and he had an open bag of gummy bears propped on the child seat of his grocery cart. It always bugs me when people eat things in the grocery store before they buy them.

The last time I saw him, he'd acted like nothing was wrong. We'd talked about the stuff we normally talked about and played video games. But after that phone call from his mom, I stopped seeing him.

I secretly hoped that it was his mom who'd made him stop coming over, but Todd always did stuff his mom didn't like. He hid candy under the floorboards in his bedroom because his mom wouldn't let him have processed sugar, and he snuck out of the house all the time. He bought *Playboys*. I'd seen him smoke weed. So I knew it wasn't because of her.

As I stood there, I made a list of all the stuff I wanted to say to him, every snarky thing that ever crossed my mind about him. But then Rebecca just looked at me and shook her head. She raised her middle finger in Todd's direction, and I smiled.

I got into a checkout line and left with the four items I needed. I know he saw me before I left, because there were only three people behind me in line. I'm pretty conspicuous. He knew it was me. He definitely knew.

I turned around for a second when I got to the exit and noticed that Todd was deliberately looking away. He didn't want to make eye contact. So I left and didn't tell anyone I'd seen him. Definitely not Maya, because then I would've had to tell her why we weren't friends anymore.

I wonder if someday he'll tell people that he had a friend who was schizophrenic and that it was too difficult to maintain the friendship because of the severity of the illness. He might get a few sad nods, and even some sympathy from strangers who think he was a nice person for trying.

I thought about keying his mom's Acura in the parking lot for a second, then just walked home instead. Rebecca did cartwheels.

DOSAGE: 4.5 mg. Begin to taper off.

MARCH 20, 2013

I feel fine.

As you know, my doctors made a decision to keep me on the drug for the time being, but to taper it off gradually. We won't be increasing the dosage or changing the medication, which is a relief. None of the really harmful side effects have manifested, and the blood tests are still inconclusive, so my mom insists that I stay on it until something else can be arranged. Not sure how familiar you are with the nasty side effects of coming off a drug you've gotten used to, but that is also a lovely spilled bucket of diarrhea.

The other doctors have mandated weekly blood and urine tests for now, but that's hardly difficult. They probably talk to you a lot, too.

One nice thing about you, Doc. You never make me pee in a cup. That's why you're my favorite.

Oh yeah, it's a blast being Jesus. Our last Stations of the Cross practice is next week. I think I've mastered the role.

I bow my head when Pontius Pilate washes his hands of my death. I let the girl playing Veronica put a cloth against my face to leave an imprint with my blood. I let two Roman soldiers nail me to a cross without screaming (because it was determined in years past that a screaming Jesus being nailed to a cross is really quite distressing to watch). Then I die with dignity after another soldier pokes me with a spear and proclaims that I truly am the Son of God, sort of like the way an old lady pokes meat at the grocery store and asks *Is this fresh?*

Dwight, as the narrator, leads the church in prayer, and I rise from the dead. So yeah, I'm ready to be Jesus. It's nice to have a distraction from the baby.

Paul is really overwhelmed with all the baby preparations. If I had to describe him, I'd say he looks a lot like a crumpled umbrella. When he leaves for work in the morning, he already looks defeated, but he also looks kind of relieved to be getting out of the house. My mom has been making him go to a bunch of classes. Lamaze. Baby first aid. Breastfeeding.

It's been a while since my mom had a baby. Obviously.

Actually, I don't think she ever thought she'd be in this position again. She thought it was going to be just me. But now that she's "with child," her friends from work and book club are throwing her a baby shower. They are handling the games, the decorations, the invitations, and everything cutesy.

I'm in charge of the desserts. Cream puffs with pink and blue filling. Tiny baby-bottle cookies. Layered carrot cake, because it's my mom's favorite. And a vast assortment of cupcakes.

Our house has become a shrine to tiny, ridiculous things. Gifts have started pouring in even though the party is still a few weeks off.

Since my mom refuses to learn the sex of the baby, everything is yellow—the color for parents who wish their babies to be sexually ambiguous and confusing for people who look anxiously into strollers expecting to know immediately what they're looking at.

It's amazing because now that we don't live in the Middle Ages, I think it would probably be a good idea to take advantage of the scientific advantages available to us. But when the doctor asked if they wanted to know the sex, my mom said that *they* wanted to be surprised.

Paul actually does *not* want to be surprised. I know for a fact that it is killing him not to know. The man lays out his clothes the night before work and folds everything in an obsessively neat pile. He wants to have a plan of action for everything, but he didn't fight my mom on this because he's suddenly become a weenie. She's become even more powerful with the pregnancy because almost everything makes her cry, and Paul can't handle that. He'd rather give her anything she wants than watch her get upset, which means they are going to have some serious discipline problems as it is with this kid.

My mom told me to invite Maya to keep me company because Paul's mom is going to be there, and even though she's forbidden from talking to anyone about me, she's still annoying as hell. So Maya is coming.

Maya came over while I was taking inventory of the kitchen. She made the list of ingredients I'd need and sat dutifully while I pulled out equipment and then tucked things away. Every so often, she'd look up at me and smile, and I'd remember that we were basically in the house alone. We didn't have Academic Team to study for anymore, no homework that needed to be done immediately, and nobody was really watching us.

It was easy to take her hand and gently pull her to my room. Easy to close the door silently behind us. But when I edged toward the bed, she shook her head and pulled me toward my desk chair instead.

She sat in my lap facing me. Her top might have come off. My pants might have been unzipped. But then the garage door opened, and we both scrambled to put clothes back on and race to the kitchen before my mom could open the door.

I cannot overstate this. I don't think I've ever been more frustrated in my life. I kept thinking that if my mom hadn't come home, would we have done it? It always feels like she's ready when we're together, but maybe that's just because I'm a guy and I've been ready since, well, I've been ready for a while.

After Maya left, Rebecca spent the next several hours throwing me casual glances that might have been smirks. She seemed pleased with herself about something. She twirled her fingers in her hair and grinned.

My mom asked me why I looked so distracted. I'm pretty sure I didn't respond.

29

DOSAGE: 4.5 mg. Same dosage. Will decrease next week.

MARCH 27, 2013

Yes, I feel fine. Normal headaches. Normal hallucinations. Nothing new. Well, that's not entirely true. Something *is* new.

Catholic schools have a lot of celebrations and recitals that require students to sacrifice valuable class time to practice. We waste an exorbitant amount of time sitting around in church so our homeroom teacher isn't embarrassed when we have to perform in front of the whole school. We are her responsibility. If we suck, she's to blame.

In this case, our entire junior class was in church. I was onstage in full costume, including the ridiculous fake crown of thorns, because this was our final dress rehearsal for the Stations of the Cross. The whole thing was a gigantic pain in the ass made worse by Sister

Catherine's insistence that I stand the entire time to try to understand our Savior's pain. Because getting a leg cramp and an itchy forehead is basically the same as being murdered in front of a crowd of people you've known your whole life.

When the last station was done, it was late in the afternoon already. All the nonessential soldiers and narrators had left for whatever sport was having practice that day. Maya had walked off with the other girls to change back into her uniform. I just stood there, messing with my beard, waiting to be excused, feeling grateful that it would all be over by next week.

Sister Catherine looked up at me approvingly and then handed me the key to the tiny storage room behind the church. It had been my responsibility to walk my elongated cross back there at the end of every practice, lock up, and drop the key in the main-office mail slot when I was done. I didn't bother changing out of my costume first. It was just as deserted as always. All the props and robes were neatly labeled in boxes. Jerseys and old sporting equipment were stacked in a heap to the side.

I rested the cross on the two pegs they'd made for me and turned to walk out when I saw Maya in the doorway. She'd changed back into her uniform already and was holding a blue sheet in her hand, her Mary Magdalene costume. I remember every detail about the way she looked in that moment, but I can't tell you what she said before she closed the door behind her and walked toward me. I remember knowing that she wanted me in the same way that I wanted her and that she wasn't going to push me away this time. Even so, I let her come to me. I wanted it to be her idea, not because I was afraid of doing anything she didn't want, but because I liked the way it felt to be chosen. Not just by anyone—by her.

We didn't speak the whole time. We undressed each other and then laughed when we realized I couldn't get my Jesus beard off without the adhesive remover, so I left it on. One of the nice things about being so much bigger than she is, is being able to pick her up like it's the easiest thing I've ever done, because it basically is. So I lifted her up and kissed her, holding her against my chest before gently setting her down on the folded costume I'd just taken off.

The really bizarre thing is that I wasn't nervous even though I knew we were both virgins. I might have been nervous if it had been planned. If I'd had more time to dwell on it. But in the moment I wasn't afraid of anything. I didn't worry about not being able to get it up. Not being able to last. Not being sexy enough for her. Not being big enough for her. I didn't worry about it because I knew I loved her, even though I hadn't told her yet.

It wasn't Hollywood sex. Nobody screamed or broke

anything, but after a while I felt her body rise and I smiled in relief. Hearing her come with short, excited breaths and watching her eyes open wide was something out of a dream. Especially when she said my name.

Having an orgasm is pretty awesome, but giving Maya an orgasm was the best moment of my life.

Even afterward, neither of us had anything to say. We just couldn't stop smiling. And it wasn't weird even though I had my hand on her boob and she had hers on my penis. We stayed like that for a long time before Maya looked at her phone and then looked at me with regret.

"Yeah, we should go," I said. We got dressed slowly and checked outside the door to make sure no one was there before walking to the front office to drop off the key. I was wearing my regular uniform again, but the Jesus beard was still firmly glued to my face. Every time Maya looked at me, her mouth broke into a grin.

When she dropped me off at home, we still hadn't talked about what had just happened, but she'd held my hand while she drove. And when she kissed me, she put her hand up to my cheek and said, "See you tomorrow?"

I nodded. We'd had sex in a storage room like it was something we did every day.

It's probably really strange that I'm telling you this. I don't know anyone else who would share details of their first time, but honestly, it doesn't feel that weird. Okay, it's weird, but maybe that's one of the nice things about not actually vocalizing these things. I'm not sure I would have ever been able to say any of this aloud to anyone. Writing it down makes it feel more remote, like I can crumple this entry up and destroy it before anyone has the chance to read it. Once words tumble out of your mouth, there's no room for editing. It's out there.

Maybe telling you this proves I can have a normal life.

DOSAGE: 4 mg. Decreased dosage.

APRIL 3, 2013

When my grandma was alive, she was the one who made my Easter basket. It always had Peeps, which I've never liked, and those big, fat supermarket jelly beans that no one likes. But she also filled it with Cadbury eggs and Reese's Peanut Butter Cups. I used to eat them Easter morning before my mom woke up.

After Grandma died, we didn't celebrate Easter any-more. It was weird enough being an only child in an Italian family, but now we're the only Italian family in the world that doesn't do anything for Easter.

This year, though, my mom forced us all to go to church. I think the thought of a heathen child suddenly makes her nervous. Limbo is supposed to be lined with the skulls of unbaptized babies.

Easter Sunday is one of the days people pretend

they're full-time Catholics even when they're not. It's the only time we've ever put on the big show, gotten dolled up, and acted like we actually agree with what's going on. It was probably better when the whole thing was in Latin.

Mass seemed longer than usual, more uncomfortable, too, since it was standing room only by the time we got there with the rest of the people who only show up on holidays. Someone stood up for my mom because she's pregnant, but Paul and I had to lean against the back wall of the church for an hour. I started getting fidgety before the homily, and I spent most of my time avoiding the stained glass. Rebecca sat off to the side of the priest where the deacon normally sits. For some reason, there was no deacon for this mass, so she had the whole bench to herself. She met my eyes and smiled.

I saw Maya there with her whole family, even her mom. Who was basically the Maya of the future. When Maya noticed me standing in the back of the church, she blushed and turned back to face the altar. I couldn't stop grinning when she did that. I couldn't help it. It wasn't the fact that she got all red and embarrassed. It was that *I* had made her blush in church. She'd been reminded of what we did in the storage room, and I knew she was just thinking about it in church. On Easter Sunday. In front of God and everyone. And I had been dressed as Jesus.

It's hard not to feel a little smug about that.

DOSAGE: 4 mg. Same dosage.

APRIL 10, 2013

The weird thing about yesterday is that I don't remember getting out of bed. I remember standing in my bedroom for a while, watching Rebecca sleep, and then walking out into the hall to stretch my legs. I was feeling twitchy.

The other weird thing is that I didn't take my phone. I realized this even before I saw the mob boss in *my* family room lounging on *my* couch with a cannoli and a cappuccino. He didn't have the same manic look on his face that he did when he opened fire at school. He actually looked pretty calm, just watching while the two boulder-sized men behind him browsed our bookshelves.

"It's late. You should be sleeping," he said.

"I also shouldn't be seeing you." I was in no mood to be lectured.

"Cannoli?" he asked, raising it to my face. It smelled delicious. That's how crazy I still am. I could smell the cappuccino and the cannoli as if I'd just bought them at a bakery or, you know, made them myself. The powdered sugar disappeared into a puff of dusty air when he took a bite, little bits falling on the rug.

"No thanks," I said.

"Your loss, kid." He stuffed the rest of it into his mouth and wiped the sugar on my great-grandmother's crocheted blanket. That irritated me for a second, and it must have shown on my face because his mouth split into a wide grin.

"You really want to yell at me for that, don't you?"

"I didn't say anything."

"You don't have to. I've never met anyone so tightly wound. How *did* you get that stick up your ass, kid?" When I didn't answer, he took a fistful of cookies and crushed them into tiny crumbs, dropping them deliberately onto the ground in front of him. This is the part where you would interrupt me and say, *But, Adam, at this point, didn't you know he was a hallucination?* Why, yes, Professor, I did. The same way I know that there are no monsters under my bed. But that doesn't mean I let my feet dangle over the edge, either. It's difficult to know anything with absolute certainty, especially with a very real hallucination staring back at me.

"How long do you think you'll be able to keep this up? Do you think your little Flip girlfriend is still gonna wanna touch your junk when she finds out you're a schizo?" I couldn't remember if "Flip" was a slur or not, but I winced.

"It didn't bother your mom," I said.

The men behind him flexed their muscles warningly, but the boss actually laughed.

"That's more like it!" he roared, wiping sugar from his lips. "We're a part of you, paisano. Every single one of us is a piece of you, and you hide us like we're trash."

"You're not real."

"Bullshit," he said. "To them maybe not. But we've always been real to you."

I didn't say anything.

"And what about her?" He tilted his head toward my bedroom, where Rebecca was sleeping. "Are you casting her out, too?"

"She doesn't make me crazy," I said.

"None of us *made* you crazy." He laughed.

"If I can't see you, I can move on with my life."

"So if you can't see us, we don't exist? I don't think that's how it works."

"I'm going to bed."

"You do that, kid. Just remember what I said. You

can't keep this up forever. The drugs can only do so much."

I walked back to my room and climbed into bed. Rebecca was still sleeping. Her hand found mine, and I squeezed. She squeezed back.

32

DOSAGE: 3.5 mg. Decreased dosage.

APRIL 17, 2013

I feel fine. For most of this week, it was just Rebecca and the choir. The rest of *them* haven't been seen for days.

How's my mom's pregnancy going? I'm a terrible son. I know I'm supposed to say that Mom is glowing. That she's never looked more beautiful. But the fact is that I saw her eat an entire Costco bag of Doritos by herself and then burst into tears, which without any context is pretty terrifying. She's also left the remote in the fridge twice in the past week. Paul says it's called "pregnancy brain," but he never says that above a whisper. Also I'm pretty sure she used to have ankles. Now her leg just shoots directly into her foot. I mentioned this to Paul, who gave me a warning look but didn't disagree.

Maya says that her mom didn't have any of those mood swings. Or cravings. She basically just looked bloated until she was ready to give birth. This confirms my belief that Maya's robotic behavior comes exclusively from her mother. Maybe she's a clone.

My mom wants me in the room when the time comes, but Paul has already said he's willing to make my excuses. Thank God for Paul. The man has grown on me. I'm not sure I could handle the emotional turmoil of the birth while still pretending everything is magical. Without throwing up. As it is, it's going to be difficult not to be repulsed by the baby when they hand it to me for the first time.

Newborns are not cute. They're hideous, squishy pink larvae that don't look like *either* parent regardless of what anyone says. Compared to the rest of the animal kingdom, human babies are fugly. I feel like I would be more emotionally attached to a baby platypus than a human.

Maya agrees with me. She says that there's a picture of her holding her two brothers after they were born and she's not smiling.

"I was afraid of them."

"Afraid of babies?" I asked.

"You just wait," she said knowledgeably. "They're fragile and horrifying. Like tiny monsters that suck the life out of you. Every noise they make means something,

and they always *need* something. Food, diapers, sleep."
She grimaced.

"So you don't want kids someday?"

"Probably not," she said. I waited for her to elaborate,
but she didn't, so I asked her why. "Because no matter
what you do, they can still get messed up anyway. There's
no guarantee that they won't do drugs or get sick or end
up hating my guts just for trying to be a good mom."

"You worry about that kind of stuff?" I was amazed.
It was also kind of refreshing to hear, in a "shit happens"
kind of way.

"If I don't have kids, I don't have to. How's your
head?"

"Fine," I lied.

She's right, though, of course. Maya may not be the
warm-and-fuzzy type. She might not even like kids. But
she always notices the little things and responds accord-
ingly like a friendly robot. She can read my moods, and
she always knows when she can get away with asking a
steady flow of questions and when it would be best to
wait for me to tell her something on my own. She may
not be nice, but she's really *good*.

And I'm not just saying that because I'm sleeping
with her.

It's been about three weeks since our first time, and

every time since then has been different. The first time, neither of us knew what we were doing. Obviously.

I don't think either of us was nervous; if Maya was, then I'd missed it completely. The second time, Maya climbed through my bedroom window again, and instead of teasing me for hours, she got into bed with me, pulled down my pajama pants, and put the condom on me herself because I was already hard. I'm not sure how a person can be so regimented in one aspect of their life and then so completely free in another. It makes no sense that Maya would color-code her notebooks and analyze my headaches and then completely lose herself in sex without worrying about our parents finding out. But in this case, I don't want her to make sense. I want her to be Maya, and I want to have sex with her.

The third time was completely different. I'm not saying that I didn't connect with Maya the first time or look into her eyes and drift off to another place, because I did that, as much as anyone can in a storage room, but this was different. We could actually study each other in daylight. It was just the two of us with no interruptions from anyone, including my imaginary friends, and I'm still not sure why they gave us privacy.

I'm not supposed to say this, but she's not always as beautiful as she was that afternoon. I'm supposed to say that she is *always* beautiful and that it doesn't matter what she's wearing, but that's one of those things that men say because it's the most correct way to lie. There are moments when Maya sort of looks like a newly hatched iguana with squinty eyes and puffy cheeks, like in the morning when we're sitting outside our first-period class, waiting for the bell to ring.

But that afternoon, she looked more beautiful tangled in my sheets than she's ever looked in clothes.

We never stopped touching each other. I developed an appreciation for body parts that don't normally get much attention. Like her wrists or the really tender spot on the back of her knee. I liked knowing I was the only one who got to touch her. There were long, comfortable silences where she ran her fingers across my stomach and let me twist my fingers in her hair. She smelled incredible, not like perfume or lotion, just like her.

I felt like I could tell her everything, like what I actually saw in church when I had to close my eyes or why I had horrible headaches and couldn't sleep sometimes. Every fear I'd ever had. In those moments I felt like she would understand and nothing would change between us, but I didn't want to tell her like this. I didn't want to tell her all that stuff when I was feeling happy. It would've ruined the feeling for both of us, and then the afternoon wouldn't have been the day I opened my heart to Maya—it would be the day she found out I was broken.

When she said she had to leave, I wouldn't let her put her clothes back on, which led to a wrestling match that gave me an unfair advantage. Poor Maya.

Mom and Paul came home about half an hour after Maya left. They'd brought pizza, and Paul and I politely ignored my mom when she insisted that two extra-larges were way too much for us, even though she finished most of one herself. Thank God for Paul or we could've starved.

That night, Maya climbed through my bedroom window, but instead of climbing into bed with me, she tilted her head toward the window and climbed back down. I followed her into the driveway and then toward the small park on the corner of our neighborhood. It was chilly out and I thought she looked cold without a sweater. She glanced back at me, flashed a grin, and started running toward the line of trees on the far side of the park. When I was younger, I wasn't allowed to venture this far alone, and for some reason that old boundary tugged at me.

I followed her to the other side of the trees, where the street curved out of the neighborhood and toward the freeway. Maya hadn't stopped running. She was ahead of me, far ahead of me, and when I called out, she didn't stop. I ran after her.

Until I saw her veer straight into traffic.

I screamed her name, but she just turned into vapor as a truck plowed through her.

It took a while before my mind could process what had happened. There had been no warning in my head that she wasn't real. I hadn't thought it was strange that she was running away from me. She was wearing her school uniform, and even that hadn't seemed out of place. The only thought in my mind had been to follow her.

What if Maya wasn't real? I climbed back through my window and spent the night thinking I had invented her. Everything in my body hurt because I was so fixated on the idea that she might not exist. I was afraid to talk to my mom about it because I didn't want her to know if my girlfriend was made up. I was almost positive my mom had asked about her before. She'd come to the house for dinner and studying. Mom knew Maya existed. She absolutely knew. The little voice in my head kept asking, *Are you sure?*

I got to school early and waited for her to show up. My head was pounding. When Maya finally arrived, I waited for someone to say something to her. Anything. I needed someone else to see her first and respond to her. Luckily, Sister Helen came into view, and I heard her say, "Good morning, Maya."

"You're going to get us in trouble if you kiss me like that at school," Maya said when I finally put her down. "There are rules, you know. You can't just go touching me whenever you want." She smirked and twisted her hand into mine.

I'm not sure what you got out of this entry. Probably that I shouldn't be left on my own and maybe that I need stronger meds, but I'd actually prefer that you thought I was just a horny teenager. If you could just pretend that's all I am, I'd really appreciate it.

DOSAGE: 3.5 mg. Same dosage. No change.

APRIL 24, 2013

Look. You don't have to try this hard. You could probably take a nap during these sessions and nobody would notice. I won't tell anyone.

I'm touched that you went out of your way to try, yet again, to connect with me, but even if I was, you know, normal, an art exhibit was a risky move. So you could have wasted your time.

My mom was really glad you took me. You should have heard the way she went on about your innovative therapy style and how you really seemed to be reaching me. I think I have to care about the art itself, though. The fact that the paintings were done by someone like me doesn't make them more beautiful and it doesn't make the artist less crazy. I almost ruined everything as usual by not appreciating the first exhibit you dragged me to.

To be fair, it was full of bent penis flowers. Huge paintings of bent, flaccid penises with crowns of petals around the tips making them look like the saddest flowers I've ever seen.

I really want to say the right thing about this stuff, so if you could just tell me what I'm supposed to be feeling, that would be awesome. I assume that I'm supposed to be comforted by the fact that these artists are able to show people what they see in their heads. Right? And because they are all schizophrenic, I'm supposed to be moved by their ability to reach beyond the limitations of their disease to create something beautiful.

The painting of the cat wearing glasses in the garden is supposed to teach me something about embracing the crazy. But what I really think is, *Who cares about this cat?* The answer is no one. No one cares about this cat. The artist barely cared about this cat.

I think I know what happened. My last entry worried you. You seemed different when you read my stuff this week. Like you were afraid I was losing my grip. But I'm not sure showing me art from other people like me is the way to go.

It's creepy.

Why do they paint so many misshapen penises with flower petal hats? And that one guy, the one who painted all the cats. That guy is seriously messed up. The thing I really want is for the artist to stand in front of his painting and tell me what the hell he was thinking. If the cat is actually a submarine and the penises are actually people, then I'd like to know about it because looking at them on their own without any explanation is stupid.

And I seriously hate when *other* people tell you what the artist was really trying to say. Like the museum curator standing in front of the painting with the bent penis flower telling everyone that it symbolizes his detachment from the world of academia after he was diagnosed.

It's a drooping flower with a penis for a stem. It could mean anything, or it could just mean he wanted to paint sad penises and used flowers to cover them up. Let the artist come out and say, *Yes, this was a way for me to express my sadness after I was forcibly removed from my teaching post at Notre Dame for showing up on campus naked.* It makes it more difficult if the artist is dead or too crazy to answer, but then we should just look at it. And that's it. We shouldn't pretend we understand.

I just want to hear it in their voice. I don't want someone else who has no idea what their work means to speak for him. He probably spent the rest of his pathetic life trying to get people to listen to him. But they wouldn't because he was crazy. So he painted instead. And rather than let him tell someone exactly what his work meant, they send some lady with a BA in art history and an ugly green blazer to do it.

But maybe you didn't bring me there for the freak show artist part. Maybe it was the other exhibit you actually brought me to see. The culinary one.

I'd never seen food like that before. The cake towers were pretty impressive. And the rows of perfect fruit tarts that looked like jewels. I can see why they belonged in an exhibit. I've never seen food look so beautiful before.

It was a lot of color. Like all the cooks and bakers had gotten high and blasted their ingredients with psychedelic paint. But I liked it. I liked the way everything was stacked precisely, like an army of food.

The thing I like most about it is that I can do it. It isn't inaccessible like most art. It was beautiful because it was real.

Anyway, thanks for taking me.

DOSAGE: 3.5 mg. Same dosage.

MAY 1, 2013

Yeah, I feel fine. Like I said, I'm better when I'm baking. It removes the distractions.

And cream puffs might sound easy, but they're actually pretty technical. Even if you get the pastry part right, you never know if you've filled them enough. I had to cut a few of them open before I knew they were okay.

And I did it with an audience. Rebecca was watching me from her kitchen stool, smiling every so often at the ingredients. She frowned when the mobsters walked right into the kitchen and let off a couple rounds into the ceiling, knocking chunks off the wall and into the sink.

"Can't ignore me forever," the mob boss said. But I kept filling the cream puffs, and he eventually moved to the corner of the room to watch the festivities.

I think you probably know that I hadn't exactly been

looking forward to this baby shower. I wasn't expected to serve food or entertain guests or participate in any of the absurd games, but the event itself was not what I'd call a good time. On the plus side, I have never seen my mom so excited for a party. And my desserts were amazing.

Paul's mom was ushered immediately into the living room with the rest of the guests before she could open her racist, homophobic mouth—that incidentally looks like a dog's anus.

She just nodded in my direction and was dragged into the midst of the celebration by my mom's friend Mauve, who was coordinating all the activities. Yes, Mauve is a ridiculous name. It will not be on my list of suggestions for the baby if it happens to be a girl. Paul's mom sat rigidly on the couch and then immediately started speaking to Janice, my mom's old boss, the nicest person in the world. I wish I could've warned her, but that would've meant going over there, and I was not willing to do that. I just had to hope that Janice's kindness would not be destroyed when it came in contact with Paul's mom.

Maya burst through the door a few minutes later, wearing quite possibly the ugliest sundress I've ever seen, which I didn't tell her. Before waving at her, I waited for my mom to say hello. I handed her a plate of cream puffs, and we watched the party unfold like visitors at some exotic zoo.

Dwight's mom walked through the door like a pale, skinny stork. She waved at both of us before joining the crowd of squealing women flocking to my mom. I told Dwight about the party and that he was more than welcome to come, too, unless he'd rather stick pins in his eyes or get diarrhea or do almost ANYTHING else. For some reason, he opted out.

Again, I had to hear about breastfeeding because my mom got a breast pump as a gift. And then someone at one end of the room criticized someone at the other end of the room for using formula, and shit was about to get real. Everyone looked uncomfortable. Even Maya, who normally didn't pay attention to such things, leaned forward and said in a low, creepy voice, "Blood in the water."

But Mauve was a professional. She chose that exact moment to start another game while my mom was opening gifts. The game was being able to identify the melted chocolate bar in the diaper. I will never understand why that was an appropriate use of chocolate.

My head twinged a little bit on and off, but nothing too terrible. Maya distracted me with questions about the guests and a few robot-like observations.

"You know, you probably aren't going to sleep much when the kid is born. They'll probably cry and wake you up. My brothers did."

"Thanks, Maya."

"And the weirdest thing is going to be how nervous you are when it's sleeping."

"What?"

"You're going to check on it every time you pass its room just to make sure it's breathing."

"Babies don't breathe?" This was a legitimate question. I wasn't exactly sure what babies were capable of.

"They breathe very softly. Sometimes you can't tell."

"Awesome."

Sometimes it's not actually a good idea to talk about this stuff with Maya. She's a little too clinical, a little too real. I don't want people to give me fluff, but I think I'd be okay if people didn't tell me directly that I'd be worried about a kid that is not mine. She could sugarcoat things a little. When I told her this, she shrugged.

"This *is* your kid," she said. "Your mom and Paul are going to rely on you way more than they would under other circumstances. You're old enough. You're responsible. You can handle it."

That was when I felt the guilt. I wasn't going to be able to help the way I was supposed to. I wasn't going to be the big brother my mom needed me to be.

Even though I've been doing really well and the drug still works, they'd never leave me alone with their baby. The kid is going to grow up knowing that I am different, and then it might even feel obligated to take care of me.

That was what I was thinking until the end of the party, and even though Maya didn't say it, I could tell she was waiting for me to tell her what was on my mind. I never did. So she changed the subject.

"Hey, the prom. You're taking me, right?" she asked, raising an eyebrow.

"Aren't *I* supposed to ask *you*?"

"I guess."

"Why didn't you let me, then?" *I'd completely forgotten about it.*

"Sorry, go ahead." She sat back, waiting.

"Well, there's no magic in it now."

She rolled her eyes. "Look, *I'm* asking you. Will you go to prom with me?"

"I'm still missing the magic, Maya."

"Don't be a jerk," she said, but her lip curled ever so slightly into a smile.

"Okay, I'll go with you."

She kissed me and called me an idiot. Then she left with a tray of desserts after saying goodbye to my mom. Paul's mom watched her leave with a raised eyebrow. She pronounced the word "Filipino" weird, slowly, making sure that every syllable hit her shriveled tongue as the word slid out of her mouth. I tried to ignore her.

Everyone loved my desserts. And everyone squealed with glee when Paul showed up "unexpectedly" with roses, which my mom graciously accepted and put into the vase that was waiting to receive them. It had been Mauve's idea, and my mom didn't argue, even though she hates flowers.

When everyone else left, Paul's mom started talking. "Well, that was a lovely turnout. We didn't have quite so many contraptions for our children when Paulie was growing up."

My mom murmured her agreement and only cringed a little when she heard her call him "Paulie." She thinks it's obnoxious when grown men still sport their cutesy baby names.

"You know," Paul's mom said in that annoying, whiny voice she adopts whenever she's about to make a point, "it's really time you start talking about living arrangements for when the baby comes." My mom and Paul were both trying to figure out how to set up the baby swing they'd just gotten, and it looked like they didn't really process what she was saying. "You can't just pretend you don't hear me."

"No one is pretending that, Mother. We're just waiting for you to make your point," Paul said.

"Where is he going to live when the baby is born?" She looked directly at me when she said it, and I swear I heard my mom hiss.

That did it.

It might have been a pleasant, laughter-filled after-noon before that moment, but that was all over now.

"I sincerely hope you're not talking about my son."

My mom is nice. Mostly. But she can get scary real quick.

"No, of course she's not," said Paul. He glared at his mother, who did not flinch.

"Like hell, I'm not," she said. "If you're going to en-danger the life of my grandchild—"

And from there it got pretty heated. Like, really heated. I didn't even have time to get angry about her accusation, because my mom immediately came unglued and my unborn brother or sister was treated to some surprisingly salty language. I was a little proud. Paul had to remove his mother from our house before my mom killed her.

I sat at the kitchen table with Mom for a while with-out saying anything. She squeezed my hand. I squeezed back. But we were silent. I think she thought that if she tried to speak, she'd cry.

Paul came back home, and my mom went directly to their bedroom to lie down without saying a word, slam-ming the door behind her.

Paul sighed and grabbed a beer, and I asked him something I knew he was probably thinking about.

"Are you worried that your kid might turn out like me?"

"Like you? No."

"Are you sure?"

"Yours is not the influence I worry about. I think it's safe to say that on her most normal day, my mother could out-crazy you."

It was the wrong thing to say, and I think he knew that when the words left his mouth, but we both laughed anyway, grateful that my mom wasn't there to ruin the moment by being offended. But somewhere in the back of my head, all I could think was, *Challenge accepted.*

DOSAGE: 3 mg. Reducing dosage to discontinue.

MAY 8, 2013

I feel fine.

One of the many reprieves from our actual education is the annual visit from the Knights of Columbus. Maya says they visit all the Catholic schools in the state, and they've been coming to St. Agatha's since she was little. There were three old men with papery skin and knobby knees from the local chapter standing together with their little navy-blue suits and lapel pins. As a Columbian Squire, Dwight had to stand at the front of the room with them, wearing his own navy-blue blazer and lapel pin. He looked mortified. Ian was standing next to him, along with a few other boys, but Ian didn't look embarrassed. He just looked bored.

It's hard to waste too much energy disliking these old guys, though. They do a lot of charity work and put a lot of money back into local businesses. They're also mostly harmless old men who are just in a club because it was something their fathers wanted them to do, and they're too ancient to cause trouble. And yet there's something. Definitely a creep factor.

I remember their signs outside our grocery store. I remember the way my mom shook her head and pushed me toward the car before one of the Knights could offer us a button. There was something my mom didn't like about them. I think it's the way they protect family values, but only families that look like theirs. I think it's also the way they like to quote Leviticus.

The oldest and frailest of the group opened his mouth to speak. For a second, I was sure that nothing but dust was going to trickle out, but he was feisty for an old guy. "We're here today," he said in a voice that sounded like every FDR recording I've ever heard, "to talk to you about becoming Columbian Squires. Or Squirettes, as the case may be." He grinned at the girl in the front row, then proceeded to tell us about the history of the organization and the essay contest they sponsor every year.

Here's my problem. I feel guilty about thinking bad things about old people no matter how much I don't like them. It's like I'm programmed to respect old age as a virtue all on its own with the exception of Paul's

evil mother. *Respect your elders.* When shouldn't it be . . .
respect everyone?

But the thing I forget when I look into their sad, pathetic, cataract-filled eyes is that being old does not make
you a good person. Old age is not, in itself, an admirable
quality. Sometimes it just means you haven't had the
sense to let anything kill you.

My mind might have already started to wander at this
point. Rebecca sat straight up and reached for my hand.
She always knew when something was going to happen
before it did. A second later, two men walked through
the door, and I understood her anxiety.

I've only seen them a handful of times. In fact, I'd
nearly forgotten what they looked like. These two hardly
ever show up when I'm alone, and they never do anything
quietly. In fact, they kicked the door open so hard that it
crashed against the opposite wall, knocking imaginary
items off the shelves. And not to sound too philosophi-
cal, but I know why these hallucinations come around.
They come around when I want to argue but can't.

They're both tall, older gentlemen in three-piece
suits. One is thin and the other is fat. And they're both
British because I guess if my subconscious is going to
win an argument it's going to be with an English accent.

The thin man is called Rupert and the fat one is Basil.

Their names popped into my head the same way they did. Quickly and without explanation.

"Right," said Rupert, leaping onto Sister Catherine's desk and kicking papers to the floor. "I can't believe they do this in a school. They should actually be learning something, yeah? Something useful."

"You'd think so," said Basil, stuffing a muffin into his mouth. "But these gentlemen look like they're half dead already. What a shame."

"God, it must be bloody awful to be that old. Imagine sitting on your shriveled man berries." Basil spat out his muffin.

"Oy, Ru. Enough. That's disgusting," said Basil.

"Just listen to them," Rupert said, his lips curling into a smile. "Knights of Columbus. I don't think I've ever heard anything more ridiculous. Do they even know who Columbus was? Not exactly a role model. And the subject of the essay is 'the real message of the Catholic Church.'" He laughed, rolling off the desk and onto the floor. "What do you think they should write about?"

"How to not get caught raping little boys?" Basil offered.

"Or how to quietly sack a pope for his secret ring of pedo priests?" Rupert shouted, swinging from the overhead lights while Basil fished a bag of candy out of his pocket.

"Yoo-hoo! Adam!" Rupert called in a high, girlish voice. "Thoughts? We wouldn't be here if you didn't have any. In fact, you probably agree with us."

This was always the worst part. The persistent hallucinations who want a reaction. Of course, you'd say that *I* was the one who wanted a reaction, since the visions belong to me. But they wouldn't leave me alone. They juggled. Took swigs of something from a flask and sang "Danny Boy." I hate that song. Rupert even dropped his pants and shook his bare ass in Sister Catherine's face.

The old man up front never stopped talking. Phrases like "your duty as young Catholics" and "defending your faith against immorality" floated across the room. His cracked and wrinkled lips continued to flap up and down while I watched the two British gentlemen destroy the classroom without turning my head. The trick was pretending to pay attention to the old guys at the front instead. The problem with that is Rupert and Basil are not to be ignored.

"You were a lot more fun when you thought we were real," said Basil, shaking his head sadly at me.

"Is that her?" Rupert whistled. He walked over to Maya's desk. "The one you, you know—" He wriggled his finger into a hole he'd made with his index finger and thumb. Both of them laughed. "And your first time you were dressed as Jesus. I applaud you, sir."

"A lovely creature, to be sure," said Basil, his belly drooping over his belt.

That was when I stood up and left the classroom, taking the bathroom pass with me. Everyone's head turned in my direction as I walked straight for the door. Maya's eyes burned into the back of my head, and I saw Ian turn toward me with interest. The old man faltered a little in his speech but picked it back up pretty quickly. Sister Catherine didn't try to stop me, but her blond eyebrows disappeared into her forehead in disapproval.

"She needs a good shag," Basil whispered, shaking his head.

I walked straight to the bathroom and splashed water on my face. Naturally, they followed me. It was too much to ask that they would give me some privacy and let me clear my head.

Rebecca leaned against the bathroom wall and glared at them.

"It's no good looking at us like that," said Rupert, sticking his tongue out at her. "Adam is verbally constipated at this school. You know it. I know it. Basil knows—" He turned around to look for him. "Really, right now?" Basil was using the urinal closest to the door.

"Had to take a leak," Basil groaned.

"Don't you get tired of keeping quiet?" Rupert asked me.

"No," I whispered.

"Ohhhh, he speaks!" Basil said. "About time."

"Please go away," I said.

"Why? So you can lie to yourself?"

"Please?" I asked again. I held on to the sides of the sink, trying to steady myself. The headaches rolled like waves against my temple. For a second, I thought I had it under control, but then I felt the acid rise in my throat as I turned and vomited all over the urinal. Rebecca leaped from where she'd been standing to put her hand on my back. Rupert rolled his eyes.

"Look," Rupert said, running his fingers through his hair. "You're too big to act like a timid mouse, my friend."

"You've got big ideas and your opinions are valid. I don't think you've said a word in class since you got here," said Basil, pulling out his candy again. I hoped he'd washed his hands.

"Please," I begged. "I can't do this here. I shouldn't be seeing you." The room started to spin again, and I knew that I was losing control. I could feel the throbbing in my temple and the rise of the vomit in my throat again. Rupert looked hurt.

"You're losing it," he said. "You'd rather keep quiet and take your drugs until there's nothing real left in you. Until everything that's beautiful and creative and interesting about you is diluted. You're pathetic."

"GET OUT!" I screamed.

It was bad timing. Some third grader had wandered into the bathroom at the exact moment that I'd screamed. It might have been startling to walk into someone shouting in a bathroom, but I imagine my size coupled with the fact that my fists came crashing down against the sink just as he walked in made it even more terrifying. For a second, he looked like he wanted to cry; then he bolted.

The door didn't even get the chance to slam shut behind him before I saw Ian staring at me blankly, then fumbling hurriedly with something in his pocket as he turned toward the puddle of puke on the urinal. He didn't say a word. He didn't even look smug. I was shaking, and his eyes were just opened wide in disgust. Maybe even fear.

Rebecca reached for my hand, and we walked out of the bathroom in silence, slamming into Ian's shoulder as we left. We didn't stop walking until we got home. It's funny how sometimes your own hallucinations can hurt you without touching you or saying anything you didn't already know. When I walked out into the hall, I could still see them both out of the corner of my eye, their suits like blurs in my vision.

Coward, they whispered.

DOSAGE: 2.5 mg. Tapering off. Monitoring Adam for negative reaction to decrease in drug.

MAY 15, 2013

Sometimes when you talk, I don't actually process what you've said until I get home. Like last week, when you asked about the prom coming up and told me how nervous you were about your first high school formal, I sort of tuned you out because I haven't had time to worry about stuff like that.

Don't feel bad. I tuned Dwight out, too, when he said he was going to ask Clare. I mean, I think I nodded or something, but I didn't actually offer anything insightful to the conversation. I might've told him that I'd see him there.

I pretended to listen to Maya talk about her dress. I think it was at that point that she told me it was going to be blue and strapless. It was the girliest conversation I'd ever had with her, but instead of appreciating it for the Loch Ness monster moment that it was, I'd ignored her, too. I nodded, kept up with the conversation, and let her believe that I was having one of my headaches, when, for the first time in months, I actually wasn't. My head felt fine.

Maya never said those things that girls usually do when they think something is wrong. The barrage of questions or the inane *Are you mad at me?* Those kinds of things would never have occurred to her because (1) a barrage of questions is more annoying to her than it is to me and (2) she knew she'd done nothing wrong.

When I got home, I opened my blinds for the first time in months and threw open my window. My mom says keeping the blinds closed was something I've done since I was a toddler. From the time I could reach the cord, I'd pulled them closed.

I sat in my desk chair and watched the people outside for a long time. In the evenings, our street is packed with people. Kids, mostly, but a lot of joggers and old ladies walking their dogs, too. It's noisy. I'd forgotten how noisy it was. The sound of feet on asphalt is irritating, and the crunch of bicycle wheels over gravel feels like nails on a chalkboard. But then I remembered that I didn't open my window to listen. I wanted to take a real look outside.

It took a few seconds to get there, but I knew it was waiting for me. Next to the trees along the sidewalk, I could see it more clearly. The blades of tall grass outside my house began to move as if tiny creatures were creeping in it. I could always find the edges of crazy if I looked hard enough.

The sun was setting, and the street I'd always tried to hide from was changing. Streetlamps flooded the concrete with orange light beneath the massive jacaranda trees that left purple crap all over the ground. Then suddenly there were no moving bodies to stare at, and the odd car that happened to glide past our driveway floated in slow motion as if the people driving through knew there was something wrong with me.

I tried to listen to them.

Why is he staring out the window like that? What is he looking at?

I'm not paranoid.

Maya sent a few more messages about her dress, but I didn't respond, which isn't like me. I'd told her earlier that I'd wear whatever tux she wanted me to. I'd pick it up before this Saturday.

But there was something different about tonight. I keep looking out at the neighborhood, waiting for something else to happen. Until finally it does.

It's subtle. None of the familiar characters charge the

streets and the voices don't start, but the ground rolls beneath my toes. I can feel it breathe. Even the darkness is intensified. Everything is alive.

The smell of star jasmine outside my window reminds me of Maya. She says it's her favorite scent in the world, and it actually does make me feel good for half a second before I remember what's going to happen to me.

It wasn't a good meeting with my doctors today. They asked a lot of the same questions, though nobody seemed to care much about my sex drive. Unlike the other 65 percent of the schizos in the study, I'm not actually getting any better, which they already know because my results indicated a weakened response to treatment. My body has started developing immunity.

They issued the final stop date. They can't advise continued treatment because of prior complications with my heart.

So I stared out the window and listened to my phone buzz with Maya's texts because I didn't want to respond. Rebecca reached out to touch my hand.

"Is it strange watching your world crumble around you, knowing there's nothing you can do about it? I imagine it's strange." It was Rupert, leaning back on my bed with a lit cigarette, looking bored, while Basil snored against the wall on the floor, scratching his balls.

"Leave him alone," said Jason.

"Why?" said Rupert. "Look at him. He's already angry. He's got so much anger in him it's trying to claw its way out." He walked over and stared into my eyes, putting both hands on my shoulders. "He wants to scream and break things."

"Well, you're not helping," Jason muttered.

"We're not supposed to help," said the mob boss, suddenly appearing next to the window. "We're not supposed to do anything. We're just here. Always here."

"I know!" I screamed. "I can't fucking take this anymore. Just stop talking! All of you! Please stop talking."

Then it was quiet and it was just me and Rebecca listening to the voices sing while I sat down to answer Maya's texts.

DOSAGE: Unknown.

MAY 22, 2013

Bad things happened.

Hospitals smell weird. Like piss and antiseptic.

I should tell you that I'm not the guy you met anymore. You know this already, but I feel compelled to tell you anyway, just so you know I know. I'm not on the same drug anymore, so I'm feeling pretty tired. This other stuff they've put me on feels weird. I wet the bed when I first got here. That's one of the cool side effects. You can't really feel it when you have to pee.

I didn't realize you'd told my mom about our silent sessions, but I guess that makes sense. She doesn't really let anyone keep secrets from her. I'm sure that even if you wanted to keep that little bit of our relationship a secret, you couldn't have. My mom knows. That's why I'm sending this entry to you as an email instead of handing it to you across your desk.

Gotta love my mom. Even when everything goes to shit, she wants me to keep seeing my therapist. It's her ongoing journey to make me whole. Probably because she feels responsible that I'm broken. "How's my boy?" she asked. Like nothing had changed.

She brought me my laptop and told me to do what I always do. I told her I normally just answer the questions you asked me during our last session together. She told me to just make questions up.

I said something like, "Well, I've made up the rest of my life. Why should this be any different?" So she started to cry and I started to cry, too. And Rebecca, who had already been crying, was a hot mess.

"I don't know what you want me to write."

"Just tell him what happened."

"Didn't you already tell him that?"

"Let him hear it from you."

"He's never actually heard—"

"Just write it, Adam."

It was the closest she's ever come to scolding me, and I could feel the wave of regret the minute she raised her voice, but eventually Paul came in and took her down the hall to get some tea. Herbal tea. She still doesn't want to have Earl Grey until after the baby is born. The caffeine, you know. Moms give up a lot of stuff for their kids.

I ended up not having to make anything up after all. Thanks for coming to visit me, by the way. I'm not exactly sure what they have me on now, but by the way you were reading my chart and shaking your head, it's really strong stuff, which is why I've been so out of it. I'm still in awe of your ability to talk while I say nothing. You still haven't given up on me. The pause after your questions is so optimistic, so courteous, it almost makes me sad. But I gotta hand it to you. The dry-erase boards were pretty crafty.

When you handed me one and started writing with the other, I was actually a little bit impressed. I mean, you probably could've done this months ago and stumbled across some huge breakthrough, but better late than never, right? Writing to you while you were sitting right in front of me was weird. Your handwriting is terrible, by the way. Also, can you let me know if this didn't actually happen?

Me: Are you real?

Doc: Yep

Me: How can I be sure?

Doc: You can't

Me: Why are you here?

Doc: Just checking on you

Me: I'm not your responsibility right now, Doc.

Doc: I know

Me: But you feel guilty?

Doc: Not the right word

Me: Afraid?

Doc: No

Me: Disappointed?

Doc: NO!

Me: Then, what?

Doc: Angry

Me: At me?

Doc: Of course not

Me: At who, then?

Doc: The universe

Me: I'm angry, too.

Doc: Do you want to talk about it?

Me: No.

When we both laughed, that was the first time I'd smiled since I got to the hospital. Thanks for that, Doc.

But maybe it's time we came to terms with the fact that I am not getting any better. The miracle drug that changed my life was not as magical as we'd all hoped.

You want to know what happened at prom, but you already know. You'd think I'd get annoyed telling you things you already know, but I'm "Lucy in the Sky with Diamonds" right now, so I'll tell you. I assume you just want me to tell you in my own words so you can close your file once and for all and mark me with a scarlet "C" for "crazy." So here goes.

I knew they were going to cut me off soon, so I saved up a bunch of ToZaPrex before prom. I can go a day without feeling the effects of a missed dose, so I'd been skipping every other day for two weeks.

I went into the back of the closet and pulled out all the doses I'd saved and took them all at once, because in my mind that would get rid of all the side effects that have been cropping up.

Mom and Paul had already decided that I couldn't go to prom. It was one of those "for your own good" moments. Mom cried and told me that I needed to tell Maya, which is probably what I should've done. Instead, I told them I'd already explained it to Maya. But there was no way I could've disappointed her like that.

I lied to everyone and went.

I had Maya pick me up while my mom was taking a nap. She didn't ask why my mom wasn't begging us to take a million pictures inside the house, which is what she would have done normally. I guess she was distracted.

We weren't exactly the epitome of cool rolling up to school in a green Odyssey, but Maya doesn't care about that stuff. She had no interest in getting a limo. Fancy crap that doesn't mean anything makes her uncomfortable, and the van was good enough. Dwight and Clare were meeting us there. Maya said we were all going to get dessert somewhere afterward.

Let's pause here to address the fact that I hadn't noticed what she was wearing or even taken the time to make sure that my tie was straight. I was busy trying not to throw up. My amazingly perceptive girlfriend didn't notice because she had concerns of her own that night. You can't blame her. Dances take a lot more effort for girls than they do for guys. Her entire day had probably been spent getting ready. I was out the door in twenty minutes while my mom had been passed out on the couch.

When we got out of the car, I walked over to put on her corsage (the one I'd hid in the back of the fridge so Mom and Paul wouldn't see) and was about to say something pointless about getting in line for pictures or putting the tickets in her purse when I stopped midsentence.

A lot of women look good in formal dresses, so it isn't really fair to say that Maya was the most beautiful girl ever in existence, but that was basically the truth. She looked like an angel.

I'll describe her for you in case you've never seen an angel and because I'm really high, and talking about angels is oddly comforting.

Somehow she'd gotten her normally bone-straight hair to fall in soft curls around her face. Her dress was pale blue and didn't have any of that gaudy sparkly crap. It was elegant and fell just off her shoulders. There was a band of shiny fabric under her breasts that tied in a bow behind her, and at the right angle, it really did look like folded wings.

And I clearly wasn't the only one who thought so. Plenty of people were turning their heads in our direction. Granted, some of them were probably muttering something about Maya needing to be saved from the giant ogre behind her, but mostly they were gasps of awe.

Did the doctors tell you that this is the first time in two days that I haven't been strapped down and sedated?

Anyway, I was okay with the fact that I'd lied to get there. I didn't know how long it would be until my mom woke up or Paul got home and realized I was gone. But I knew they wouldn't embarrass me when they got there. They'd just show up, wait in the back of the gym, and throw daggers at me with their eyes. That would be the worst of their wrath. I just didn't realize that it was *my* reaction I needed to worry about.

Maya pretended that she didn't care about dances and dresses and girlie stuff, but she had a death grip on my hand. She was happy.

Can that be where the story ends?

I feel like since these are my entries and I clearly have problems that this should be the point when the story ends because we were both happy and everything was fine, even though it actually wasn't. If I'm good enough, do you think we could make it so that everything that happened after that moment was a hallucination? Maybe we could all pretend that prom hadn't happened yet, right? If everyone pretends together, that makes it real.

I can almost see your face. The sad smile that you've adopted whenever you read something that clearly provides evidence to have me locked up forever. You should work on keeping your expression neutral. I would be happier if you didn't care at all. I'd like a lot more people to provide neutral expressions, actually. I think they would be closer to what they're actually feeling. No one can possibly care that much.

I *am* crazy, but even I know that can't be where the story ends. I started feeling the effects of the drugs a few minutes after I took them. It had been too much all at once. Maya thought I was just nervous because I don't like crowds, but I was sweating and having a difficult time breathing. That was a warning. I should have already been heading to a hospital, but then a slow dance came on, and the part of me that wanted to be a normal guy pulled Maya onto the dance floor. We waved at Dwight and Clare, who were swaying awkwardly nearby.

Catholic school dances are pretty tame. There were streamers and glow-in-the-dark stars hanging from the ceiling, and the DJ they'd hired had a strobe light flashing against the wall and monitors projecting neon images around the dance floor. Once in a while a nun would push two kids apart and whisper something about leaving space between them for the Holy Spirit. Still, Maya leaned into me and I tried to forget that I wasn't normal. She almost made it happen, but they found me eventually.

All of my imaginary friends were there. That feels nicer than calling them hallucinations, doesn't it? I could see them all lined up against the wall while I was dancing with Maya. They all wore somber expressions on their faces, and I realized that they were sad for me. None of them wanted to be what I was afraid of. They didn't even want to be there.

It was the voices.

I heard something break while I was dancing with Maya. A glass, maybe, but I couldn't see where it was. I jerked my head in the direction of the sound and must have accidentally tugged Maya along with me, because she asked me if I was okay.

"I'm fine."

"C'mon. Let's sit down. You're not fine," she said.

"No, I want to keep dancing."

"You have a headache. We should sit for a minute."

"I'm fine."

I let her drag me to a table at the back of the auditorium as a roar that sounded like crashing waves at the beach filled my ears and knocked the wind out of me. I fell into the closest chair.

"We're leaving. Something is wrong. You're sweating."

"I'm fine. Nothing is wrong." But even as I said this, I knew she would never believe me. It's one thing for her to not know exactly what was wrong with me and another thing entirely for her to be oblivious to a problem. And my hands were already shaking when I noticed Ian standing at the other end of the dance floor, staring at us.

Just then, the monitors that lined the dance floor stopped flashing, and an entirely different visual began playing on all ten screens as the music stopped playing. It was a video of me.

I was illuminated on the screens, vomiting onto a urinal, slamming my hands against the sink, screaming "GET OUT" at the third grader, my eyes unfocused and my hands shaking. Someone had recorded the whole thing.

And suddenly I couldn't breathe.

"Adam?" Maya whispered, trying to put her hand on my back. "What's going on?"

Then the voices started.

What is he waiting for? He has to run. Everyone knows now. He's got to get out.

Ian had done this. He'd always hinted that he knew my secret, but now he had evidence. And the rest of the school could see it, too. There I was. A freak on display for everyone to see. For Maya to see.

I saw Ian run toward us, and my body began to vibrate. I just knew I had to move, but before I could do anything, he turned into something else, something dark and unnatural that slithered across the floor and launched itself into my chest.

It's hard for me to give details about what happened next, so I'll tell you what my mom told me. Apparently, she'd heard it from Sister Catherine, who came to pray over me when I first got here. I was out of it, so I don't really remember.

Hearing it from my mom was worse than remembering it myself. I had to keep asking for details until she told me the whole story.

"You screamed for a long time before you would let anyone get near you," she said.

I don't have any memory of this, so it's weird that I can still burn with shame, isn't it? "Who was I screaming at?"

"I don't know." But I could tell by the way she'd said it that she meant she knew I was screaming at nothing.

"Did I hurt anyone?"

"No," she whispered, touching my face.

"Liar," I said. She'd made her trademark lemon face.

"You pushed her down, sweetheart. But she's fine."

I remembered sticking out my arm to stop something from running into me. I shoved it away from me and ran in the opposite direction as fast as I could. I'd had no idea it was Maya.

I lost control and pushed Maya to the ground. And while I was busy losing my mind, there was no one to tell her what was going on. No one to explain.

"Does she know?" I asked. My mom nodded, wiping tears off my cheek. She held my hand for a long time.

"I told her, honey."

I cried for a long time, but I didn't get mad about it. I didn't tell my mom it wasn't her place to tell Maya anything. She'd given me plenty of opportunities to tell her myself, and I couldn't do it, so in the end, my mom did my dirty work. All I'd wanted was for her to keep telling me that Maya was okay and that I didn't hurt her. It seemed like every time she said it, it wasn't real and I needed to hear it again. She didn't say anything else about the prom. About taking the drugs when I wasn't supposed to. About lying to her and Paul and putting myself in danger. I told you that my mom is the kind of person who makes you feel important. And she is. But she's also the kind of person who makes you want to feel powerless because it's nice to be taken care of.

After a while she told me that the baby was kicking

and asked me if I wanted to talk to her belly. I just shook my head and asked her where Paul was. He was waiting in the hall. Giving us some privacy.

It must be hard to hold someone's hand while they're in restraints. And on the list of shitty things you have to do as a parent, telling your kid what happened when he lost his mind is pretty high up there.

My mom said that Maya had tried to visit when I was in the ICU, but it was against hospital rules. Family only. When they transferred me here, I still didn't want to see her. Actually, I just didn't want her to see me.

But I did see her mom.

Remember I told you she's a nurse? She came in to check my IVs but didn't say a word while she worked. I didn't want to say anything to her, but I couldn't stop myself. She had Maya's eyes.

"Can you tell her I'm sorry?" I whispered to her.

"You can tell her yourself."

"I can't see her again. Not like this."

She looked at me.

"Nothing you have is impeding your speech. You can tell her yourself."

"Look," I said. "Now you know what I have. You understand better than she does. You know there is no cure. I'm going to be messed up for the rest of my life. Am I really the kind of boyfriend you want for her?"

She considered me for a moment and then turned to leave with her tray of instruments.

"*That,*" she said, "is not up to me."

Then she closed the door behind her, leaving me alone to fully appreciate how warm and fuzzy Maya was compared to her mom.

Later, I could remember fragments of what had happened. Even in my delirious, drug-soaked mind, I remember the look on Maya's face when I pushed her. Funny how you can remember something small like that. The way her face sort of dropped when she fell. Her eyes were wide, and her hands were stretched out at either side of her body as she looked up at me from the ground. I must have looked like a monster. That was when I ran.

I didn't get far, obviously. I'm surprised I even made it up to the bathroom between the church and the hall to throw up. The words were still scrawled on the bathroom wall in there, and it made me wonder if they couldn't get them cleaned off or if the nuns left them there as a reminder:

JESUS LOVES YOU.

Don't be a homo.

That fit somehow. Together, it sounds like a conditional phrase. Separately, it sounds like one guy being nice and another guy being an asshole. But the most surprising thing about it was the way it could be twisted with one extra word. JESUS LOVES YOU BUT DON'T BE A HOMO. It was all in how you read it.

"Jesus loves you" basically says "Come as you are." "Don't be a homo" passes judgment. They contradict each other, like everything else in life, I guess. You'll hear one thing that gives you hope and another thing that takes it away.

Be who you are.

But not that. Anything but that.

That was what I was thinking when I threw up again. But after that, I was definitely gone.

There were footsteps. I remember that Rebecca held my hand in the ambulance, and I thought it was odd that I couldn't hear my mom. I heard Paul instead. Somewhere in the back of my mind, I knew he was crying.

He kept saying that everything was going to be okay. "I'll call your mom when we get to the hospital. You don't have anything to worry about. I'm here."

I let him take my hand because, really, what else was I going to do? He took the hand Rebecca was already holding. She looked at me for a moment, as if willing me to say something. The thing we both knew I wanted to ask.

"You're not real, are you?"

It's stupid. But when Rebecca shook her head, I felt heavy, like I was learning it for the first time.

"I'm real, Adam."

Of course Paul was the one to answer. I didn't say anything else. I just let him squeeze my hand.

I bet you think that all these months of therapy and experimental treatment have been a waste since I wound up crazier than before. If it makes you feel any better, you still got paid. And it *was* nice of you to visit me in the hospital. I said that already, didn't I? It's also nice that I can always tell that you're not a hallucination. Nothing in my imagination would conjure up that hair or those pants.

MAY 29, 2013

Coward.

That was what I was thinking.

Yes, Maya is still calling and sending texts and trying to visit, but I haven't responded and I told the nurses not to let her in. Not since the last time, when I woke up to find her sitting next to my bed.

I was pretty high on whatever they'd given me, so for a minute I didn't know what to think. I figured it would be best to check.

"Are you real?" I asked.

"Yes," she said. I could tell she'd been crying. Her eyes were red and she was wringing her hands in her lap like she was trying to get blood pumping to her fingers. Then she looked at me again and I saw it. That tiny flicker of understanding that hadn't been there before prom. That little spark of knowledge that meant she knew now. And there was nothing I could do to take it back.

"How long have you known there was something wrong with me?" I asked. We both knew there was no point in denying it. She wiped the corners of her eyes with her sleeve.

"I didn't know what it was," she said. "I just noticed the headaches. And sometimes you had this look like you were . . . seeing things." She looked up at me and my throat burned, but no matter how much I wanted to, I was not going to cry in front of her. I wasn't. "Why didn't you tell me?" she asked.

"I didn't want you to know I'm broken." I was suddenly very aware of how I must look to her. My eyes had been bloodshot the day before. I wondered if they still were. My hair was matted to one side, and I could feel a sticky patch of sweat on the back of my neck.

"But how could you keep this a secret from me?" she asked.

"I kept it a secret from everyone."

"I thought . . ." She paused. "I thought I was different."

She searched my face for something. Sanity. Understanding. I'm not sure what, but when she looked down again and started to cry, I knew she hadn't found it. I took a deep breath.

"No," I said. "You're not different. You were always going to be afraid of me."

"Adam, that isn't fai—"

"Fair?" I shouted. "Do you really think any of this is fair? Do you think fair has anything to do with what's wrong with me?"

She shook her head as the tears rolled down her cheeks. I'd scared her. I knew the minute I raised my voice. She flinched. And I realized I was the one who'd made her do that. I really was a monster.

"Please, Adam. Let's just talk about this when you're feeling better. You've been through a lot."

"Feeling better," I muttered. "Crazy isn't something you ever recover from, Maya."

"Just let me help."

"No!" I shouted, again deliberately. "I've already let you do too much."

"Please, Adam . . . ," she said, and for the first time, she actually sounded as small as she looked.

"Just go," I said. "It's better if you just leave."

It didn't matter that I could suddenly hear all the voices talking at once or that the bullets from the mobsters' guns made me flinch in my bed. I pushed the button for the nurse, and Maya got up and walked out, still crying.

That was when I realized that I hadn't actually been broken until then. Until I'd made her cry.

I was actually relieved that my mom told Maya. It meant I didn't have to. I don't have to see her again if

I don't want to. I can even pretend I never saw her. It doesn't matter in the long run. I'm not good for her anyway.

It's sweet that your questions are still pretty stupid. You asked me to tell you what the voices are saying. That sounds like something my mom wants to know. And I'm not sure I can tell you because sometimes it's not even words. Sometimes it's just scratchy noises that turn into nothing. Sometimes the voices just sound angry and I can't really translate the sound. Even Rebecca is different.

I'll be in the hospital for a few more days, and she seems really anxious about it. She hides a lot when people walk into the room. I tell her no one can see her, but she just shakes her head.

The good thing about this place is that I can sleep again. Glorious sleep. I'd forgotten how good it feels to just let yourself die for ten hours. The only shitty part is waking up.

Yeah, I am distraught about not going back to school. Horribly distraught. It tears me up inside that I don't have to sit through another sanctimonious little lecture about make-believe spirits and people who cut themselves for God.

No, I'm not sad. I'm not a weeping pile of shit. I don't feel sorry for myself and I don't have any intention of telling you what I'm actually thinking right now because (1) I don't know what you're going to do with that information, and (2) I don't want to.

I'm back home, which you already know. Dwight showed up at my house on Monday wearing his tennis clothes, looking pale as usual.

"Do you want to serve first?" he asked.

I just stared at him.

"Hello?" Dwight said.

"Dude, I can't go out and play tennis today. Didn't your mom tell you . . . everything?" I knew our moms had spoken already, but it was a weird moment. *No, I can't come outside to play. I'm crazy right now.*

"She did."

"Then why are you here?"

"It's Monday. We play tennis on Mondays." He put his backpack down on the floor and started pulling things out of it.

"Okay, but you have no idea—"

"Actually, I do."

"Then why are you here?"

"It's Monday," he repeated as if nothing had happened and it was the most obvious answer in the world.

"And I am a schizophrenic nutcase who has hallucinations and hears voices."

"I know. My mom told me." He raised his eyebrows.

"Dwight, I'm not going out to play tennis."

"Good," he said. "That's why I brought this." He lifted a Wii console out of his backpack and starting plugging it into our TV in the family room. "We'll play here."

"I suck at video games, dude."

"You also kind of suck at tennis. Do you want to serve first?"

Before I could say anything else, he turned on the game and handed me a white controller. I stared at it for about twenty seconds before taking it from him.

So we played tennis in my family room for a while. Jason sat behind us, his bare ass nestled into the couch cushions. Rebecca sat next to him. Both of them watched our game like it was the most amazing match they'd ever seen in their lives.

Then we ate Oreos and Dwight packed up his stuff. We didn't say another word about me being crazy. It was almost like it didn't matter.

I miss baking. All the knives and sharp objects have been removed and are hiding in some undisclosed location. Like a witness protection program.

Everything they think I might use to hurt myself with is gone. I'm not sure what they thought I was going to do with my pastry brush, but that's gone, too.

They've been ordering out every night because Mom can't be on her feet for long. Pizza, Thai, Italian. It's not bad, but I liked making my own food. I liked picking out ingredients. It made me happy. I get why I can't. I understand. I just wish there was something else I could do. I feel useless, which was why I snapped at Paul.

Don't be surprised. It's insulting to both of us. I'm not one of those brave people who suffer in silence. When I'm miserable, everybody knows it. I make sure of that. He was trying to explain why I couldn't make dinner, and I think I was telling him that the food he'd given me was poisoned. He asked me why I thought he would do such a thing.

"Because you're not my father. Your kid will be normal and perfect, and nothing will be wrong with him. Why the hell would you want someone like me in the picture? I'd poison me, too!"

Yelling at Paul made me realize that I was a douche bag for a number of reasons. The first one being that I still had not responded to any of Maya's messages since her hospital visit. My mom has so far respected my wishes and told her that I don't want to see anyone. But I knew what I needed to do. And even though emailing it to her was pretty chickenshit, it was the best I could do given the circumstances.

Dear Maya,

I'm sorry. There's nothing I can say to make this better, but I wanted to tell you anyway.

I never wanted you to know because I didn't want you to be afraid. It was selfish, but I couldn't stand the thought of you acting differently, being careful. Especially since I was the one who should've been careful. It was wrong to fall in love with you, and I should have known that from the beginning. No drug was ever going to fix me.

I shouldn't have kept anything from you. You deserve better and I really hope you get it.

I love you.

Adam

It was the first time I'd ever told her that I loved her. I am such a jerk.

When I hit Send, I pretended I was writing to someone I'd never met before. It almost worked for a while. I sat down on the floor of my bedroom next to Rebecca and Rupert and Basil and a few familiar hallucinations that don't have names. Jason leaned against my closet door, and the mob boss sat in my desk chair, staring at me intently, because he'd never sit on the floor.

I wanted to tell them that they weren't real. I wanted

to shout at them and blame them for my losing Maya, but I was just too tired.

"Hey, Ru?" I said.

"Yeah, mate?" he asked, leaning in.

"Can you guys sing to me?"

My voices had left, and I wasn't sure when they'd be back. I wasn't even sure if Rupert and Basil would take requests or if they could sing anything other than "Danny Boy." I don't know much about the personal lives of my pretend people. But I asked because it was what I wanted, and I thought, *What the hell?* I was just going to feel all of it. Everything I could reach.

So I hummed along while Rupert sang a song called "The Parting Glass." Something I'd heard in an old movie once. Basil whistled. Rebecca held my hand. And for the first time, the mob boss didn't try to shoot anything.

JUNE 5, 2013

Sure, I feel fine. My mom is still making me write to you even though our in-person sessions are over. I thought insomnia was the worst thing about the miracle drug, but I would gladly take insomnia over the walking-dead shit they gave me. I was so tired I didn't even register that Maya had marched into our house until she was standing right in front of me. She looked different from how I remembered. There was something slightly off about her, like she could burst into flames at any moment. But that might've been the drugs.

Paul and my mom came running when she started shouting. Well, Paul came running. My mom sort of waddled down the hallway, holding her belly with both hands.

I'd never actually seen Maya this angry before. If it hadn't been so terrifying, it would have been beautiful.

"You didn't let me choose," she said.

I didn't say anything because I was sure she wasn't real. Paul was the one who asked her what she was doing. She just put her hand up, demanding silence, and Paul obeyed. It was hard not to be impressed by that. Then she turned back to me and repeated herself.

"You didn't let me choose."

"Choose what?"

"You just assumed that you knew what I wanted."

"Maya, it's not that simple."

"It doesn't matter."

"How could it not matter?"

"Adam, you are the biggest asshole I've ever met in my life!" she shouted.

"I know."

That stopped her for a second. I could tell she was really looking for a fight. But I had no reason to argue with her. And to be honest, hearing her swear was more shocking than hearing her yell.

"You lied to me."

"I'm sorry," I said.

"Don't be sorry. Just don't do the thing you have to be sorry for."

"Well. That doesn't—"

"I am still talking."

She looked a little possessed. Out of the corner of my eye, I could see my mom easing herself into a chair at the kitchen table while Paul leaned against the fridge. I had been counting on them to lead Maya out of the house with my apologies, but it looked like they were going to make me handle this myself. Privacy was out of the question.

"Why didn't you tell me?" I think at this point I pathetically looked at my mother, who shook her head and then looked at the floor. *You're on your own.*

"C'mon, Maya. You know why. I told you why."

"I deserve better than a lame excuse and an email, Adam. Tell me."

"I can't explain it." That was a lie, but I didn't want to be honest.

"Try," she said. Her lips were a straight line across her face. So I tried.

"You know about the experimental drug I was on? The one my mom told you about."

She nodded.

"I thought that if it worked, I'd never have to tell you the truth."

"And the truth is?"

"I'm probably always going to see things I shouldn't and hear things I shouldn't, and the drugs aren't always going to work. It's possible that none of them are going to work as well as the experimental one did, and I can't take that drug anymore because it is too dangerous. I'll be on multiple treatments for a while until they find the right balance. . . . And I might never be okay."

"They'll find the right balance eventually. We can handle this."

"It isn't fair for me to ask you to handle this."

She didn't even seem to care that my mom and Paul were still in the room. I'd forgotten how good it felt to kiss her, and part of me hadn't realized until that moment how much I'd missed her. She pushed the hair out of my face when we broke apart.

"I'm not asking for fair. Nobody gets fair. And who says it's up to you to decide what I can handle?" she asked.

"Me."

"Well, you're an idiot."

"Maya—"

"In the email, you said you loved me. Is that true?" I wanted to say no. I should have said no. But I couldn't lie to her anymore.

"Yes."

"Then how about that's all that matters right now, because I love you, too."

Then I said perhaps the dumbest thing I've ever said.

"I don't care if you're not real."

Does any of this make sense to you? I know we've stopped meeting for now and we might stop having regular sessions altogether until my other doctors create a cocktail that works for me, but I can't help but wonder what you actually think of everything I've told you. I can't say that these therapy sessions have actually helped me, but then again I haven't been doing them properly. So I can't say they've really hurt, either.

JUNE 12, 2013

"What do you see?" That's Maya's new favorite question.

"Nothing."

"Are you sure?"

"No. Of course I'm not sure. I'm crazy."

"Would you tell me if you saw something?"

"Probably." She hates when I answer like that.

"And the voices. Do you hear them now?"

"Yeah."

"What do they sound like?"

"Right now they sound like you."

"Idiot."

"You know, part of me thought you'd be nicer to me now that you know there's something wrong with me."

"Well, then that makes you crazy *and* stupid."

My girlfriend is not sweet. She's not the type to bake me cookies or agree with everything I say in a sweet, singsongy voice. She does still spend a lot of time talking about things that aren't exactly helpful. But she shows up every day after school and leans up against me while she does homework. Sometimes she doesn't say anything. She just works. And every so often she'll look at me and squint as if she's trying to see the fog of crazy drifting out of my ears. When she can't, she goes back to whatever she was doing.

I feel guilty letting her love me. Big surprise, I know. Don't tell me I shouldn't, and for Christ's sake, don't tell me that nobody "lets" someone love him. Because I do. I let her love me the way a girl lets a guy buy her dinner. I don't fight it. I just accept that it's going to happen, and I just sit back and let it. Because I need her more than I've ever needed anything. That's unhealthy, right? You're supposed to say that's unhealthy. Go ahead. I'll pretend you're saying it.

Every now and then, I'll casually mention sex because why not? I'm already an asshole. I might as well throw that out there, too. Just so she knows everything is working properly and we could, you know, if she wanted.

But she doesn't want to. Not until we find the right drug. And she's right, but still. It was worth a shot and it makes this quest for finding the perfect drug even more desperate.

She promised me nothing had changed, and for the

most part, she was right. She didn't treat me differently, but she did stop asking about my headaches. Now she does research on the latest drugs and compares notes with my mom, which is weird.

I won't tell you I feel fine today, because I don't, but it could be worse.

It's nice to hear "I love you" from someone who doesn't have to be here.

Today was a bad day. I yelled at Paul again for no reason. I couldn't understand why I was so angry. Angry enough to scream obscenities at a man who hasn't done anything wrong. The voices kept saying, *Maybe we should think about sending him to a place that can handle him.* But Paul didn't say anything like that this time.

I could see that I hurt him, but I didn't care. I was shaking, and he felt like a stranger in my house. He didn't love me or want what's best for me. He just wanted me to be quiet.

My mom walked in later and left a letter on my desk next to the peanut butter and jelly sandwich she made for me hours earlier. She wasn't supposed to be walking around—her doctor had put her on modified bed rest— but Paul was out picking up groceries, so she walked in quickly, kissed me on my forehead, and left.

She knew I wasn't in the mood to talk. I hadn't been in the mood to do anything lately. And I wasn't really in the mood to read, either, but I wanted to know what the letter said.

It was a few months old, dated December 20, 2012, and it was from Paul to the Archdiocese:

> To begin with, I should not be writing this letter. The diocese has not produced a scrap of legal documentation giving you the right to expose the mental illness of a minor with no violent history. You have relied instead on prejudice and fear to prove your point. I would advise you to be careful; those are quickly becoming the hallmarks of the Catholic Church.
>
> I have nothing but sadness in my heart for the people of Newtown, Connecticut. They are victims of a senseless crime carried out by a lost soul. My pity for the shooter extends only as far as a wish that he had received the proper medical attention he so desperately needed, but it certainly does not condone or excuse his actions.
>
> I have already explained in previous letters the lengths to which my family has gone to treat this illness and to fully understand the depth of Adam's medical needs. There has been

no misrepresentation of fact. Every step of the treatment has been dutifully reported, not because we were required to do so by law, but because it is in Adam's best interest to have the adults in his life as informed as possible.

You have threatened, yes, threatened to expel Adam because one among you has already revealed confidential information to a parent in a position of power, someone who feels that the issue of schizophrenia needs to be publicly addressed.

Perhaps they think it would be appropriate to force Adam out of school or raise the issue of his attendance to a vote? Or perhaps they won't be satisfied until he is caged off from the others like a beast in a wildlife exhibit.

I met Adam when he was eleven years old. He could have rejected me completely, but he didn't. By letting me into his life, he taught me that being a parent means becoming what your children need most. Right now, my son needs me to protect him from narrow-minded people motivated by fear.

I have faith that you will find the guidance you seek and respond justly in this matter.

God bless,
Paul Tivoli

Partner, SKINNER, BOLTON, HORROCKS & TIVOLI

Before you ask me what the letter means to me, I'll just tell you that it isn't actually a big deal that I cried, because I cry a lot now. The new drug they gave me is strong, and the most common side effects are lethargy, emotional outbursts, and a depleted sex drive. So tears are normal, but I still didn't expect the letter to affect me like that. He'd never called me that before. His son. Like I belonged to him.

My mom was asleep by the time I made it out of my room, but Paul was up. He was always up late these days.

I watched him make himself a peanut butter and jelly sandwich and realized that was the extent of his ability to feed himself. He didn't even line up the bread when he smooshed the pieces together. Like a toddler left without supervision.

When he noticed me standing in the doorway, he said "hey" as if I hadn't screamed at him for nothing earlier that day. As if I hadn't done anything other than walk into the kitchen. I said hey back. Then nothing. For a few seconds, I stood there, completely aware of how crazy I looked. Completely unnerved by how normal Paul looked with his untucked shirt and half-assed sandwich.

He sliced it diagonally and handed me half on a napkin. I accepted and we ate in silence. When I was done, I pulled his letter out of my pocket and slid it across the counter toward him.

"I'm sorry," I said.

I'd meant to say *I'm sorry about earlier,* but I decided on an all-encompassing sorry instead. I'm sorry I'm crazy. Sorry I yelled at you. Sorry no one taught you how to make a sandwich. I'm sorry this isn't easier.

He considered me for a moment, then let out a breath and smiled.

"It's okay, Adam."

And for a minute, I felt like it was. He squeezed my shoulder and went to bed.

I realized my mom was right. Meals should mean something. Even Paul's crappy PB&J.

JUNE 19, 2013

I wasn't in the room when she was born. Paul made my excuses because he's a good guy, and Mom was too distracted to notice who was in the room anyway. For a while I sat in the waiting room with the she-beast, Paul's mom.

She told anyone who would listen that she was waiting for her first grandbaby, like a nice old lady. They'd smile, offer their congratulations and say how sweet that was, and walk away. Then, when nobody was looking, she'd throw an ugly glare in my direction that was supposed to make me feel bad for being alive. But it didn't. I just smiled at her.

"Can you hear them?" I whispered.

"Hear who?" she said, looking around to make sure no one was listening.

"The angels. They're singing again. And they are so beautiful. Can't you see them?" Then I gave her my best creepy psycho face. Like Nicolas Cage in basically every movie he's ever done.

She didn't say a word after that. It was the first time I was happy to be crazy.

I was wrong, by the way. Other babies are ugly, shapeless masses of flesh. But not her.

Paul put her in my arms right away. Beautiful, tiny, and pink.

She was screaming her head off when Paul gave her to me, but the second I looked at her, she just knew. She knew exactly who I was. And it didn't matter so much that the room smelled weird or that Paul's mom was looking anxiously from the baby and back to her son and miming that someone should get her the hell away from me. We were together, and there was something awesome about that. Being her big brother, I mean. It's funny how quickly you can love a person.

Paul's mom proclaimed that she looked just like Paul, and I was in a good mood, so I didn't call her a moron.

Maya showed up a few hours later to see her. She didn't want to hold her, but she didn't seem repulsed, either. High praise. She put her finger into the tiny fist and smiled.

"What's her name?"

"Sabrina," I said. Maya liked that. It was just the right

amount of lovely, the kind of name she could grow into. I didn't really want to think about her growing into it, because it was unsettling, the thought of her becoming a little girl. It meant she would become a woman someday, too. And maybe things would change. I wanted to remember the way she was looking at me in that moment.

Dwight came by and brought Sabrina a giant teddy bear with a pink tutu. He held her for twenty minutes straight, talking to her the whole time until she needed a diaper change, and then he handed her back to my mom. He didn't look grossed out about it, though. He was in awe, and I didn't blame him.

My hallucinations visited, too, which was kind of annoying, but they didn't mean any harm. They just sort of hung out behind my mom's bed and made faces at the baby. She couldn't see them, but I didn't want to spoil their fun. I wasn't really in the mood to ruin anyone's good time. I was too tired to do that.

I thought my visions might change after the new drug, but they didn't. The only one that still seemed different was Rebecca. She jerked around a lot, and whenever someone shut a window or opened a door, she hid behind whatever she was closest to. When the baby started crying, she dropped to the floor and covered her ears.

I wanted to reach out and say something to her, maybe

tell her to not be afraid, but everyone was in the room, and whatever drug I was on at the moment seemed to be doing the trick. I knew I shouldn't speak to her, but I still felt guilty watching her fall to the ground. She looked so lonely.

Ian showed up at my house today.

I thought he might come eventually. Everyone knew he was the one who'd played the video at the prom, so he was probably getting pressure to *do something*.

When I saw him standing at the door, I wanted to hit him. Even though it had already been a month since it happened, I was still angry. I wanted to squash his pathetic little face in my hands and shove him over my porch railing, but part of me thought he might not be real.

"Yes?" I said.

"I came to apologize," Ian said, holding a paper bag in his hand and shifting uncomfortably. It was the first time I'd ever seen him uncomfortable, but I had a strong feeling he wasn't a hallucination.

"Okay," I said.

"Okay?" he asked.

"I mean go ahead," I said. He grimaced. "Are you?" I asked.

"Am I what?"

"Sorry."

"Why the hell else would I be here?"

I looked out at the car on the curb and the woman behind the front seat. "Did she make you come?" I asked, indicating the woman who was obviously his mom.

"No. I just don't have a license yet," Ian said. I didn't want my face to show surprise at this piece of information. I didn't ask why because I didn't really want to have anything in common with him.

"So, why exactly are you here?" I asked again, pretending I hadn't heard him the first time.

"To apologize," he said breathlessly. He looked *really* uncomfortable now, and I took a certain degree of satisfaction in watching him squirm.

"Yeah, you haven't done that yet," I said, leaning against the doorframe and looking out onto the street.

"Look, I was just trying to get you back," Ian said. "I didn't know about the drugs you were on. I didn't know about any of that."

"But you knew what I had? My 'condition'?"

He nodded.

"And you thought it would be funny to broadcast my breakdown to the whole school?" I asked. My voice was surprisingly calm, given my initial desire to hurt him.

"No, it's not like that—" he started to say.

"And my stepdad isn't pressing charges against you. I

told him to drop it. So if you're here because you're worried about that—"

"That's not why I'm here," Ian said, cutting me off this time but not meeting my eyes.

"Why the fuck *are* you here, Ian?" I asked. He flinched and I suppressed the urge to smile.

"Because I meant to get you, but I didn't mean for it to go like that. I didn't mean for anybody to go to the hospital. It went too far. And I'm sorry." His voice dropped as the apology leaked out of his mouth. "Okay?" He thrust the paper bag he'd been carrying into my hands. I opened it.

"Cookies?" I asked, my mouth hanging open in shock. "Did *you* bake these?"

Nothing could have prepared me for that moment. He'd actually baked me cookies to show me he was sorry. It was the equivalent of him getting down on his knees and begging for forgiveness. It was worse than seeing him naked.

And fuck, I wanted to laugh.

"Your girlfriend told me to bake them," Ian said.

"But—she what?" I was completely blown away by this.

Just then Dwight pulled up in his mom's Toyota, hitting the curb just enough to make an annoying squeaky noise as the rims grazed the concrete. He got out of the car, and upon seeing Ian, he headed straight for us and positioned himself squarely at my side.

"What's he doing here?" Dwight asked me, as if Ian weren't standing there.

"He came to apologize," I said, opening the brown paper bag to show Dwight the cookies. He reached in and grabbed one, glaring at Ian as he bit into it.

"Well, that was it," Ian muttered, walking back to the car as fast as humanly possible.

"Ian," I called out just as he reached the door. "Thanks."

He nodded.

"And, dude," said Dwight, "stick to swimming. Your cookies taste like shit."

Dwight tried to look innocent as Ian got into his car. "What? I got your back, man."

I sent Maya a text later that day.

Me: You told Ian he should bake me cookies?

Maya: Actually when he came to talk to me I told him that he should rot in hell with maggots slithering through his eye sockets and leeches attached to his armpits and that it still wouldn't make up for what he did to you

Me: Hm. Guess he got that wrong then

Maya: Then I said he should apologize and if he had any humanity left in him he would bake you cookies.

The weirdness of this statement was staggering.

Me: WHY

Maya: (1) He made fun of you for baking me cookies on Valentine's Day and said they were an apology for being cheap

I remembered this.

Maya: and (2) He had to think of you while he baked you cookies.

Me: Um . . . yeah. That's weird.

Maya: No, it's perfect. Anybody can just eat a cookie. But if you bake for someone, you're forced to think about that person while you're baking. And he should think about you and feel ashamed of himself

Me: Okay.

Maya: You still think it's weird, right?

Me: Yeah but the maggots and leeches thing sounds pretty badass.

JUNE 26, 2013

I remember when *The Half-Blood Prince* came out and having to wrap my head around it. It was the angriest I've ever been. Well, the angriest I've ever been while reading a story. Like Harry hadn't been through enough already.

At least Dumbledore came back toward the end of the last book. Remember? Maybe you don't. It was at King's Cross station. That hallucination where he told Harry he had a choice. And then, when Harry asked if it was real or if everything was just happening inside his head, he said: "Of course it is happening inside your head, Harry, but why on earth should that mean that it is not real?"

He's right, isn't he? It doesn't really matter that no one else can see what I see. That doesn't make my experiences any less real.

Real is subjective. There are a lot of things that aren't actually *real* to everyone. Pain, for example. It's only real to the one experiencing it. Everyone else has to take your word for it.

It's nice to know that Sabrina is never going to question whether something is real. She's never going to find herself fighting imaginary creatures or talking to people who aren't there, and before you ask me how I know that, I'll tell you. It's because crazies recognize each other. Like a secret membership to a club nobody wants to join. We can see when someone is one of us. And Sabrina is not.

You're probably going to say that she's a baby and there's no way anyone will be able to tell until she's older. I *know* she's a baby. But there's something solid about her. Maybe it's the fact that she's Paul's daughter. She's got his unruffled personality already. And I can tell she knows that people are depending on her to be okay. That's a lot of pressure for a baby. I hope she doesn't feel it already. I'd like to think that for now she only feels the love. From everyone. Especially me.

The rest can come later, when she's ready for it. She'll be tough enough to handle it.

They're getting excited. You know, all the people no one can see. I won't call them hallucinations anymore. It doesn't really seem fair. They're just corporeally challenged. Learned that from Harry Potter, too. J. K. Rowling is a fucking genius. Anyone who doesn't think so is crazy.

If we were still having our sessions, you'd probably be asking why the people no one else can see are getting excited. You always wanted to know more about them. I think they're probably excited because they know something is happening to me. They feel it the way old people can feel rain in their bones.

Rupert and Basil are sitting with their legs crossed, laughing at jokes no one else can hear, and the mob boss is standing with his gun, looking at the door. Only Rebecca looks nervous. She keeps looking at me pleadingly with her eyes full of tears. But she always looks like that these days. And that's when I take her hand and tell her that everything is going to be okay, even if other people are around. And that's because of something Maya said when I told her about all of my imaginary friends.

"So Rebecca is you, essentially?" Maya asked, straightening her glasses and lifting her head from my computer screen for the first time in hours. School is out, but she's been researching other clinical drug trials since she found out about me.

"Yeah, I guess she's essentially me," I said.

"Is she here now?" Maya asked.

"Yep." Rebecca was doing a handstand against the wall while Maya sat at my desk.

"If she's afraid and you need to comfort her, just do

it," she said. The green flecks in her eyes looked brighter than usual.

"What if people are around? They'll know there's something wrong with me," I said.

"You are the only one who can make her feel better," she said, ignoring my question.

"Maya, she's not real!" I said, trying not to laugh.

"She needs you. And she's a part of you," Maya said simply. "Stop punishing yourself for something you can't control."

"You mean stop punishing *her.*"

"It's the same thing, remember?" Maya said. "Anyway, tell her it's going to be okay." Then she added, "Because I'm right here."

I reached out for her fingertips and smiled. "Guess we're lucky, then," I said.

"Yes," she conceded, turning back to the monitor. "You are."

I looked at her, letting her words hit me properly. Then I smiled.

"'I love that you get cold when it's seventy-one degrees out,'" I said. "'I love that it takes you an hour and a half to order a sandwich. I love that you get a little crinkle above your nose when you're looking at me like I'm nuts—'" She interrupted me with a kiss before I could finish the movie line, and her face softened.

"I love you, too," she said, touching my face. "Now shut up for a minute so I can read."

I want you to know that I get that reading whatever is on my mind isn't an easy thing for someone else to do. It probably changes you a little, having to get into people's heads every day. I get it, and I'm glad that you were here to read this stuff because being me is actually pretty lonely.

I always made it seem like our sessions were this huge drag that I wanted to avoid, but that was a lie. They weren't. And neither were you.

You're good at your job. And even though I didn't work out the way everyone wanted me to, it wasn't your fault. It's not anybody's fault. I could've been a lot worse without you. So thanks.

Oh, and you know what I completely forgot to tell you? I sent in my Knights of Columbus essay.

Ha. Yeah, when I got back from the hospital, the packet arrived in the mail, and even though I knew I wasn't going back to that school, I thought I'd do that one last piece of homework. Just for fun. I didn't even tell Maya I was sending it in.

So I answered their stupid question—"What is the real message of the Catholic Church?"—with a little something I picked up at St. Agatha's.

JESUS LOVES YOU.

Don't be a homo.

Rupert and Basil couldn't stop laughing when they read that. There was a definite note of pride when they clapped me on the back.

And that's all I wrote. Damn, I would have loved to have seen their wrinkly old prune faces when they read it. Of course, even if they told any of my teachers about it, the nuns would just say that I was mentally ill and they should pray for me. I prefer "crazy" to "mentally ill." Sounds more dignified.

When I walked into your office this afternoon, I hope I didn't freak you out. I hope that you don't think I started talking to you because I've given up. Because I haven't. I just realized that I don't have any reason to fight you anymore. I don't have to pretend that I don't need you or that I'm too damaged.

I also realize that all I said out loud today was, "Good news. I'm still crazy, so you still have a job." But, you know, baby steps.

Alas, adventure calls, Doc. It's been real.

But actually, I've got a train to catch.

See you on Wednesday, right?

Author's Note

I am not a doctor, and ToZaPrex is not a real drug. Adam's experience is loosely based on documented symptoms of schizophrenia, but a great deal of creative license was taken to describe his auditory and visual hallucinations. While Adam's story is fiction, schizophrenia is a serious and complicated disorder that affects millions of people worldwide. It is important to note that the vast majority of people battling this mental illness are *not* violent and do *not* pose a danger to others. The disorder can manifest itself in a variety of ways, and though there is no cure, there are promising treatments available.

If you are suffering from a mental illness and need to talk to someone, please contact the National Alliance on Mental Illness:

1-800-950-NAMI (6264) or info@nami.org

Do not be afraid to ask for help if you need it. You are not alone.

ACKNOWLEDGMENTS

And let the thank-yous begin. . . .

Heather Flaherty, my fantastic agent, who rescued me from a life of insurance customer service in my sad little cubicle. Your candor, kindness, and unwavering support have changed my life forever.

Chelsea Eberly, my magnificent editor, who fought valiantly for Adam from the beginning, and all the talented people at Random House who helped make this book possible.

My first editing council: Kortney Bolton, Katie Skinner, Michael Skinner, Laura Horrocks, Brooke Tabshouri, Britt Booth, and Jennifer Lowe. Thank you for being my first readers. Your feedback gave me the courage to send Adam's story out into the world.

Jennifer Longo and Peter Brown Hoffmeister, for reading during the final edits and supporting Adam's story with kind words!

Dr. Edward Fang and Dr. Nancy Fang, for patiently

answering my questions about clinical trials and intensive therapy.

My in-laws, Doug and Margaret, whose love and support despite my lack of common sense have made me a semifunctional adult. *Mahalo* for saving me from myself!

My parents, Mike and Linda, for reading me stories and filling my head with lovely nonsense, so much so that I'm now unfit to do anything practical. Many thanks, parental units. ☺

And of course, my husband, Doug, and my daughter, Alexandria, for making my life beautiful.

ABOUT THE AUTHOR

JULIA WALTON received an MFA in creative writing from Chapman University. When she's not reading or baking cookies, she's indulging in her profound love of Swedish Fish, mechanical pencils, and hobbit-sized breakfasts. Julia lives in Huntington Beach, California, with her husband and daughter. Follow her on Twitter at @JWaltonwrites.